Grady

THE MCCADE DRAGON BOOK 3

KATHI S. BARTON

This is a work of fiction. Names, characters, places, and incidents are products of the author's imagination or are used fictitiously and are not to be construed as real. Any resemblance to actual events, locations, organizations, or persons, living or dead, is entirely coincidental.

World Castle Publishing, LLC
Pensacola, Florida

Copyright © Kathi S. Barton 2017
Paperback ISBN: 978162896151
eBook ISBN: 9781629896168
First Edition World Castle Publishing, LLC, January 9, 2017
http://www.worldcastlepublishing.com

Licensing Notes

Cover: Karen Fuller
Editor: Maxine Bringenberg

PROLOGUE

The queen, his queen, sat upon her throne and cried. Warrior, the only name he'd ever been given, moved closer to her, close enough that she could touch him should she wish. He gave her warmth, something he could tell she needed in this cold room, even though the hearth was overflowing with flames. The jewels, which were as much a part of her as the crown that she wore, glistened in the evening fires. And she wore them like the queen she was.

"We're to be put out, my friend. Whatever shall I do if I have no home, nor any place to house my people? They will surely die without food and shelter." He had no answer for her. Warrior thought she knew this too. But it made him feel good to know that his queen thought of the others in her keep before her own troubles. "He took it all from me. All of it. And for what, pray tell? Because he could? Because it made him feel like a king? I made him one, and he has done this to us. He thinks to take this all from me for another woman. One that will have nothing once he tires of her as well."

Warrior looked up at her when she began to pace the large room. Not much remained now, not like the riches that had been here centuries ago. Once there had been large tapestries, and long tables with bejeweled ornaments upon them. Paintings had adorned the halls of ancestors that had lived and died to make this castle the strong fortress that it was. Blades had hung along the walls, their nicks and mars in the steel telling their own stories. Riches beyond what any man could have in one lifetime had been abundant, yet the new king, the one that had been chosen for his lady, would have more, took more. Or he would kill to get it.

Babes had been born here, and as adults they had died in the same bed that they'd taken their first breath in. This place had bred queens that fought beside their men until death. And now it was in near ruin because of greed.

Warrior wanted to help her in some way, but wasn't sure what he could do. The ring on her finger flashed, and he was saddened that someone else would wear his gift to her. The jewelry he'd forged for her was the only thing that the king had not been able to find and sell off. She had done well with that at least, making sure that it was held in the family for future generations.

"The other dragons, have you told them to scatter?" He told her that they had all gone into hiding, save him. "You should have left with them, Warrior. I love you most of all, and should you be captured, then I feel all will be lost."

"I will not leave you, my queen. Without you, there would be no us." Warrior sat up when the doors opened behind them. The little boy, Caelin, came to him and climbed up on his back. A seat was there, forever, for the queen to use when she surveyed her kingdom. But little Caelin, he knew that he'd be just as welcome. "Come, my queen. Sit upon my back and let me take you someplace safe."

"No. You must be safe. For my son." He started to tell her that without her, none of them would ever be safe. "I have a plan. A good one, but I need you to help me with it. It'll work. You'll see. Caelin and his childrens' children will be safe because of it."

She told him of her plan to gather him into the jewels to keep him safe for her son. Also how doing this would keep the jewelry for them, the only thing that was of value she had left save the little boy. By separating the jewels like this, no one person would own the dragon, her dragon.

"I do not understand how my being magically separated will help your child. I can do more harm as myself than most armies can defeat."

She held her son in her arms now. Her mind, he knew, was seeing beyond what they were looking at now. The ability of sight, even her own demise, was a gift or a curse that she held to herself. Not even her husband, the traitor, knew about it.

"Many generations from now my son's children will have the pieces. And when they do, all of them will make you whole again." They both looked at the sleeping child. "Many will be broken by the curse that I shall put upon these jewels. There will be lives taken, children unborn, until the right generation comes along and makes it work. But when the right family is gathered, when they love harder than any other, there will be riches beyond their wildest dreams. Jewels and long life. There will be dragons again, too. The queen, one beyond what I am to you now, will rule you all once more as you darken the skies again."

It took them well into the next day for the magic to work. Warrior watched over her and the small boy as he got weaker; each part of Warrior that she took to add to the jewels that he'd forged for her made him less and less. He would not have it any other way, not when she was so determined to give this for her child. When there was nothing left of him but a single spark, as she called it, he felt her tears as they fell upon his back as she sat upon it one last time.

"I know that you cannot fly, my friend, but I should like to sit upon your back as I did so many times before." Caelin was there too, his little body ready to leave the castle and all that he knew when the time came. They both looked at the door, the one that was even now splintering with the weight of the monsters on the other side that would kill her. "It is time."

Warrior knew that the child would be safe. His queen had told him over and over that he would grow to be an old man; there would be a great many scars upon his body from his strength as a warrior, too. And he would sire many children, strong sons to take his seed and name until it was time to come forth again.

"Go. Now." Her son seemed to understand that his mother was putting his life before hers. He stood watching her before falling into her arms once again to have her wrap around him, just once more. And when he ran, leaving the castle and the grounds forever, they both knew that he'd be the one that saved them. "Are you ready, my friend?"

"I am, my queen."

The sound of the men on the other side did not bother them overly much. They both knew that what was to happen now would be something the men would never understand. And when she said the words over them, Warrior felt the earth move beneath him, and the castle walls shake with the power of her magic.

Thank you my warrior, my friend. See to them when the time is right.

Warrior knew not where he was. There was magic all around him, his body tight in the jewels that he'd made so long ago. And when he opened his eyes he saw the men standing in the room where he'd been only moments before, their armor as clean and bright as the morning sun. He looked at the man who had caused this all, his king.

"What mean you that you cannot find him? He is a dragon, as big as the walls that hold this monstrosity up. Find him, and my lady wife." The men scattered and Warrior laughed. The man still had no idea that he'd born a son of the queen. She'd kept the boy safe by not sharing who the child was with anyone but herself and him. "The man that brings me her head on a platter will be rich tonight. I want her and all that she stands for dead."

When he felt himself move, he knew that the king had found him and had picked the item up. The necklace. The last piece, one that could not be taken away and hidden when his last spark was put inside it. He eyed the man that had caused a kingdom to fall and wished him dead.

'Tis not his fault he is a fool. Perhaps it is, but he is a bigger fool than I thought him to be if he thinks to win this day. He smiled at the sound of his lady queen's voice. *I had no idea that I'd join you here. It is very cramped, is it not?*

It is. But we are safe here. He will not harm us now. She said nothing and he wanted to turn to her, but knew that he could not move. *My lady, he cannot harm us, correct?*

Nay, we are beyond his wrath now, but he will try. This day he will present us to his lady wife, his new lover. And when she complains that the necklace is too large for her, he will break us apart. I will no longer be able to speak to you, not until the rest of you is with me. He asked if she had known this before. *Nay, I did not. It wasn't until he touched us that I knew. He now has her belly filled with his child, one that he is as yet unaware of.* She laughed then.

What have you done, my lady? She told him that he would

have no sons born of him ever again. There would be one born of their union, but he'd not be of his seed. *You have done this? From here?*

Yes. When she moved over his spark, he felt it and was warmed by it. *My child will be the only son he has, and he is yet not aware of him. His father will be aware of him one day, when Caelin finds his sire and cuts his head from his body. But for now, Caelin is safe.*

She told him to sleep and he had no choice in the matter. As his eyes were closing, he saw her then, the lady that would wear him for a time. Warrior had no idea what to expect, but he knew as surely as he was inside the necklace with his queen, he would protect the lady with him as best he could. Warrior wished for time to go by quickly so that he might see his queen again.

CHAPTER 1

Grady looked at the inventory sheet and then in the trailer that had backed up to his building an hour ago. His delivery was not only early by a week, but someone had royally fucked up what he was to receive. He wasn't sure what he was supposed to do about it, either. He saw Kenton coming toward him with Dalton, and waved them both over. He needed witnesses, he supposed, and what better people to help him out than these two. Handing the sheet to his brother, he explained what was going on.

"I didn't order all this. I mean, I ordered some of the inventory here, but not in the quantity that I've gotten." Kenton looked in the back of the trailer and asked him what was his. "All of it, according to the inventory sheet. And even though there is about ten times the amount I actually ordered, the prices are all wrong. Like, instead of charging me seventy dollars for something, it's seven cents. Someone messed up."

"Did you call the company?" He nodded at Dalton. "And I'm assuming by the look on your face that not only did they tell you that they don't make mistakes, but to unload the truck and put your shit away. What did they tell you to do now that you've pointed it out to them?"

"Well, not quite like that, but that's pretty much what

11

they said. I tried to point out to them that I was charged only one percent of the cost of each item, and the guy hung up on me. Didn't even try to make it right. And every time I called back to get this figured out, they told me that they don't make mistakes. Who says shit like that? Everyone makes mistakes." Grady looked into the dark truck again. "I can't afford this much equipment if they ever get off their asses and figure this out."

The driver, a big burly man, came toward them. He had a phone to his ear and paperwork in his other hand. Grady warned his brothers to not breathe if they could avoid it, but he laughed when Kenton backed up. The man had not bathed in what Grady thought was at least a month. He was a nice guy, really, but stank to high heaven. The man closed his phone with a loud snapping sound and grinned at him.

"I got ahold of the shipping department. They said to tell you that they don't make mistakes like that. I told them I was looking right at the paperwork now and that they had, and they told me just to unload and get on back to the shop." The man laughed. "I don't know about you, buddy, but I'd sure like for someone to make a mistake like this in my favor. You got yourself a deal of a lifetime, I'd say."

"I can't afford this if they decide to check and find the inventory is missing." The guy told him it wasn't his problem. "Not mine either. What happens if I take this entire load, as you said, and it comes up that I stole it? Then what?"

The driver was shaking his head even as Grady finished speaking. "See the inventory on this here sheet?" Grady nodded and so did his brothers. "Okay, I'm to deliver to you this list. It's all got numbers on it, each and every box, that corresponds with the number on your packing list you got from me. And on this list, it has a breakdown of each piece, like how many you are getting and the price you gotta pay them for the privilege of getting it. I don't care about the cost...not my department. But what I care about, and this is something you should be aware of too, is that you sign that you got what's on here at this price. It's in writing. And so you know, each and every call that goes in that place, good or bad, is recorded at a third location. You covered your ass well by calling and trying to get some help."

"So you're telling me to shut up and take this." The man nodded and jumped into the truck. No small feat either, seeing that the man was at least sixty or so and had more than a little belly. "I really am not equipped to take this much right now. Does that matter?"

"Nope. You'll take it or I'll have to take it back to the warehouse. Once it's there, what do you think is going to happen to your future orders?" The man nodded when Grady said he'd not get any more orders, no matter that it wasn't his fault. "That's about right. Heard tell of a guy who didn't want to take a shipment because he was painting the walls in his back room or some shit. Well, there were no more shipments to his place, and about a month or so later, he was done. They went and messed up, but they can be right vicious when they get their asses handed to them in even the littlest of ways."

There were other companies that he could order from, Grady knew this. Some of them were closer than this company had been, but none of them were as good. Nor as reliable. Usually reliable anyway. Their ratings on their products were top notch, and he had really gotten a good price. Well, a better one now, but they were inexpensive even before this fuck up.

Instead of saying anything else—not that he knew what he'd say—he helped unload the truck, and Dalton and Kenton pulled some of the inventory off as well. The billing should have been about ten thousand dollars on just what he'd ordered, but as it was, he'd only been charged one hundred and eleven dollars. For nearly ten times the number of things he'd expected, too. Grady was either going to have one hell of a profit or was going to go to jail for theft.

It took them four hours to get the truck bed empty. It had been scary there for a bit when he realized he really didn't have room for it all. But Kenton made a few calls and the building next to his, one that Lewis owned, was opened up and the rest stored there. Grady was trying his best not to freak out when the truck pulled away. He didn't even have his first shelf put up yet.

"We'll help you." He looked at Kenton when he spoke. "We all will. And I'll see if I can get some pack to come and help as well. I'm betting with enough screwdrivers and men that know how to use them, we can have it done by tomorrow."

Ralph Donavan had taken over the pack when Douglas Parker had stepped down to become a full time attorney for the family. He left the pack in good hands, and when Ralph had come to Kenton about finding more work for his family and the pack, they'd gladly used who they could, even having them do a lot of the renovations to the other buildings around the district. And from it, several businesses had sprung up, like the new construction company, Pack Construction, as well as a firm that came in and painted entire houses in a single day. It was great seeing the town cleaned up.

Emma and Lewis brought them food at around seven that night. It had been a slow start, getting things going to where he knew they could do it, but Grady was looking around the front showroom with pride by the time they were calling it quits. In no time they had not only the shelves up the way he wanted, but there was someone sanding his hardwood floors and his office was nearly set up. He was, he figured, about a week ahead of schedule now. And with the inventory that he was still a little afraid of being in trouble over, he thought that he'd be well on his way to making his dream work for him.

It was well after nine when he made his way home. His house was coming along as well. The house had been sitting empty for a little while and things had gotten a little mussed. Having it nearly empty, he'd decided to get things spruced up. Not a great deal, but it had needed an overhaul. Painting. New carpets, and the kitchen updated. It had cost him a good amount, but since he'd only paid thirty-seven cents for the place, he knew he was still ahead of the game. He'd even hired a cook and housekeeper.

"Sir. We've held dinner for you should you like some. It's only soup and sandwiches, as we heard that you were working." He told Rachel, his housekeeper, that he would take a little. "Very good. Also, Walker said that your room has been finished, and we've put the items in the guest bathroom as you have requested. Any more word about the young lady that is coming here?"

"Not yet." The bowl of hot soup and a thick chicken sandwich were set before him. He was eating the last bites when Walker joined him. "I heard that the guest room is ready now, as well as mine? You've done a great job, you and your wife. I don't know what I'd do without the two of you here."

Walker grinned. "Thank you, sir. It has been a pleasure working with you so far. And yes, it looks very much like a woman already resides there. Miss Emma, she said to tell you that you did well."

He'd told his family what Caelin had told him…that she was coming. They still had no idea what she had nor who she was, but they knew from updates that she was on her way.

15

Caelin was getting more and more frustrated with her daily, it seemed. When he felt the touch of someone at his mind, Grady smiled when he realized immediately who it was. Grady made his way to his room to shower and hit the bed as the dragon told him about his future mate.

There is not a stronger willed woman in the world than this one. I think she is doing things this way to thwart my efforts in helping her. Just today she told me to go away, that she was fine. I do not think she's fine at all. I have told her over and over that I can help her, but she keeps telling me that she has no need for me. Grady asked him if she was still coming here. *Yes. And I'd not be the least bit surprised if she —*

Grady felt his body tense and turned off the water he'd just switched on. Whatever had startled the dragon, he knew that it couldn't be good. "What is it? Is she hurt? Do you need me to go find her?"

There is a child. He asked him what he meant. *Within her. She is with child. I know not the sex of the babe, but she is most assuredly with child. I can feel her concern for it, her fear that someone might hurt her. She still has not taken the jewel that she has to her body, but it is close enough that I can feel her emotions now.*

"How is she...? Never mind. Just tell me if she's all right. I can deal with that if she's not harmed." Caelin said nothing for several minutes, and Grady waited. He'd learned that to rush the dragon only made things harder for someone to understand. He'd get frustrated with you and his sentences would become less coherent. Finally, he'd had enough waiting. "Caelin?"

She has finally put the torque on her arm, my lord. And now, not only am I able to talk to her, I can tell that she is carrying a son. Grady said nothing. He wasn't sure what he could have said at this point. *I should like for you to go to your car, sir, and find her.*

As I learn where she is, I'll let you know. But please head north. She is safe for now, but I fear that she will not be for very long. There are others after her besides the dragon slayers.

"All right."

He started out of his room only to return to get some of the blankets that had been put in the chest at the bottom of his bed. He called to Kenton, telling him what he'd just found out.

I'm gathering my bag up now. Caelin just let me know that you might need me. Grady was out the door and into his car before he realized that he needed to slow down, take a few breaths. *Mom is on her way to your house. She said she'd get things ready.*

Grady had no idea what that meant, but sat there for a few more minutes before he thought he could drive. His mate was coming to him, and she was pregnant. He took some time to empty his mind and breathe then started the car. As he made his way to Kenton's house, he knew that he was being overly careful. He was freaking the fuck out right now, and wasn't going to have an accident before he got to her.

Kenton opened the driver's side door as soon as he got there. Grady gladly slid over to allow him to drive.

You need to head to a place called Middletown. Kenton said that he knew where that was. *She is staying in the Economy Lodge along the highway. I do not know her room number, I'm sorry, but she needs you to be there soon. As I said, she is well for now, but harmed. I fear that someone else will come for her if she does not have help.*

"We're two and a half hours away, Caelin. Do you think she will she need us sooner?" Caelin said that she did not, but soon. "Is she in labor? Do I need to call an ambulance?"

Nay, she has been hurt otherwise, a cut, but you can fix that easily enough. I cannot tell as yet how. The child is well, as is she,

17

but there are wounds to her body that need to be cared for. Grady asked him how he knew she was hurting. *Because she told me so. I can see into her mind now. Let me look.*

While they waited, Grady looked at Kenton and then the speedometer. When he asked him if he wanted them all dead, he felt the car slow. He figured he'd get them there sooner at ninety-six, but not safely. Kenton stretched his neck before speaking.

"I'm nervous." Grady said he was as well. "She's your mate, I know that, but what do you think of her having another man's child?"

"Should I think of that?" To be honest, Grady hadn't let that part sink in yet. A baby? He had no idea, but he'd seen Jorden with his son and figured it wasn't that big of a deal. "I don't know a thing about her or the child. For all I know she was raped and got pregnant that way. Or perhaps she's a widow. I don't know what to think. Or even if I should."

"I never thought of it that way. I should have. I see it a lot. I just never expected a woman, one of our mates, to come to us in that way. It's all right, but just unexpected." Grady looked out the front window as things raced by them going in the opposite direction. "Whatever happens, we'll be here for you."

"I know that."

Grady let his mind wander. He wasn't entirely sure what he was supposed to do with a child. He had been thinking of his mate and her coming forever, even before the dragon told him about her, and he had this fairy tale vision of the way things would go. He was pretty sure, after hearing Caelin talk about her, that he was going to have to revisit his thoughts. She was going to be a hellion, he knew it. Frowning, Grady thought this might be harder than he had imagined it would be. But regardless, he was going to make it work for them both.

~~~

Harper tried her best not to bleed on the bed. She'd wrapped a wet towel around her arm, but it wasn't doing much. She looked at the coverlet and decided that the blood couldn't make it any worse. It was the ugliest thing she'd ever seen, even for a cheap hotel room. Looking around at the broken dresser, she wondered who the fuck was going to pay for this. The man who had tried to force his way into her room was going to think twice about trying to take her on again. At least she hoped so. And that too freaked her out just a little, how he'd flown from the room like he'd been jerked by an unseen string.

Harper Bailey had been going for a few weeks now, even before she'd found the stupid bracelet—which wasn't a bracelet at all, she'd been told—and this.... Well, she wasn't sure she believed it was a dragon that spoke to her, but he said he was. But she only had to return it to the rightful owner and that would be the end of it. Or so she hoped. The dragon, it seemed, had more rules to follow.

All she'd done was pick it up off the floor to take it to the lost and found at the place where she was living. A place much like this hotel, cheap and with too much character for her tastes. It was all she could afford at the moment, thanks to her sister and brother-in-law.

If she'd been home none of this would have mattered. But her sister, Winnie, had people waiting for her to return so that she could be taken to another place, and who knew what would be done to her this time. Harper was pretty sure they wouldn't give her a nice piece of pie to enjoy, like she was craving.

19

Her sister, her loving bitch of a sister, was suing her. Then there was the paper she wanted her to sign, as well as what she demanded that Harper do with her child. Winnie had done this to her, had her kidnapped and held against her will while some doctors drugged and impregnated her. Then this piece of jewelry came along.

As soon as it brushed over her fingers, she nearly screamed when this voice started talking to her. The thing, the voice of a dragon, he told her, had caused her to check over her shoulder every five minutes since she'd picked the thing up. It would not shut up about someone or some group chasing her. It had been her plan to take this thing — a torque, he'd called it — to the McCades and be done with the lot of them.

Harper had thought at first that her head had been playing tricks on her. She'd been having these weird ass dreams for a while now about a man, and him turning into something else. She supposed it was a dragon...it was huge, but her mind had shied away from what he'd become and now she could hear voices. Or at least one voice. Harper thought she could no longer blame it on being huge with this kid.

Looking down at her belly, she wondered not for the first time what she was going to do when the baby was finally here. She wasn't even sure how to hold a baby, much less care for one on a constant basis. This was all Winnie's fault. And now she and her husband were suing her because they didn't want the child any longer, and they wanted the hard earned money back that they'd spent to make her this way.

Her sister, Winnie, and her husband, Jake Patrick, had wanted a child. Wanted one, they had told her, more than they did anything else, so people would think them perfect. And they were prepared to take one into their home and raise it in a way that people would see them as no longer a perfect couple, but the perfect family. Love, a word that she'd never heard Winnie use, was never mentioned regarding the child, nor that they'd care for it because they wanted to. They just needed it to look good.

Of course, they *were* the most faultless couple she'd ever known, even if Winnie didn't point that out to her every time she saw her. Winnie and Jake were both professionals, had a good place to live, and seemed to be on top of the world. All the things that Harper just had never really cared about. And that pissed her sister off too, how Harper didn't have her life together, which Winnie did. Nor did she have a real job. Harper, on more than one occasion, had told them that she was self-employed and had a nice savings account. But that didn't matter to either of them, because Harper wasn't as pretty or as special—their words, not hers—as they were.

Oh sure, she had a good home…a house that she owned, not an apartment like theirs. There was money in her bank account all the time because she didn't spend it on clothing, going out to eat, or keeping up with the neighbors. When she could get to it, she had money anyway.

Winnie, in an effort to make sure that Harper didn't run off with her money, had someone put a freeze on her personal account recently. Her reasoning had been that Harper would flee if she could and not repay her. Not that she was going to, but Jake was an attorney and that was how it was done. It had been impossible for her to get money from that account and live, but lucky for Harper, she had two accounts. Her personal account was frozen, but she had a business account that she could dip into when necessary. And it had become very necessary as the weeks, then months, had gone by.

Harper was a professional too, she thought. Not one that went to an office building every day, or sat behind a desk for

21

endless hours. She was a professional potter. And it paid well for her, too. But neither Winnie nor Jake thought it was a real job, and told her countless times that she needed to find one that paid her weekly and had health insurance. Which, she had pointed out just as many times, she also had.

Then out of the blue about a year ago, Winnie had called and asked her to come to dinner, they had some things they wanted to discuss with her. Winnie wanted to talk to her about something important, she'd told her, and that she expected her to not only be on time, but to dress properly. Harper told them that she had some things to finish up but could come in a week, and that she'd wear what she wanted or she wasn't coming. In the end, Winnie agreed.

Harper showed up on the day that had been set up, dressed in her jeans and T-shirt, just daring her sister to say something. She had been surprised at first, then leery, when both of them had been nice to her, almost pleasant, as well as not demanding.

Winnie wasn't really a nice person, even on her best days. And she'd never even tried to be close to Harper when they were growing up. After their mom had been killed, Winnie had simply tossed her aside and moved on with her life as if she'd not had a sister, much less one that needed family in her life.

So there she'd been in their picture perfect apartment in their near perfect neighborhood, wondering what the fuck she'd been invited there for. Then, after having a dinner that was catered for three people, they *retired* to the living room. Harper waited for them to get on with whatever they had on their minds.

They were planning on having a child, Winnie explained. But they were just too busy, their lives just too perfect, to take the time out now to make one, and they thought that she should help them.

"Help you? I don't know if you know this or not, Winnie, but it takes a male and a female to have a child. And even if I had a male in my life, I have absolutely no idea how I'm supposed to help you two have a kid." Harper wasn't sure what they thought she could have done for them...she'd known less about babies then than the very little that she knew now. Winnie just waved her off.

"Oh, but you will. You see, Jake has this partnership coming up. I have my career going the way I want it. Everything is just perfect, as you can see. We just want a child of our own to show off, but not all the messy work to get there." Harper asked her how messy she thought a kid would be after it was actually born. "Oh, we'll have nannies for that. And help. But with our lifestyle, we don't have time for being pregnant. That's why we wanted to talk to you. To tell you how you're going to do this for us."

Harper was younger than Winnie by almost five years. But there always seemed to be decades between them, both in life and years. Harper sat there, on their expensive couch in their equally expensive room, and tried to think what the fuck her sister was talking about. How she was going to do what, her mind kept rolling around. But Winnie seemed to think that Harper understood as she sat across from her, smiling and nodding her head.

"I don't understand what this has to do with me, nor how you expect me to help you. Just adopt if you don't have time to be pregnant. People do it all the time Though I have to say, I doubt you'll have any more time than you think you do now for a kid. Friends of mine, even with live in help, are constantly exhausted." Harper had nearly laughed at the expression on

Jake's face when she said that to him. "There are hundreds of children out there that you can mold into whatever shape you want them. Including people like you two are."

"No, that won't work for us. We've talked it over, and we don't want someone else's issues or problems. We want a child of our own. One we help create. Or you create for us." Harper had looked at Jake and then back at her sister, still not understanding. "It's not like you have a real job or anything, Harper. And we'd pay you. Besides, your body can take this better than mine, what with all that extra fat you have on you. I've worked hard at looking like this, and I don't want to mess with my money maker."

Harper tried her best not to let the fact that her sister still thought she was lazy and didn't work because she didn't have a boss hurt her. Nor did she let her see how painful her words were, about not just her body but how it mattered little to her that Harper was happy with herself. Harper didn't wear fancy dresses or high heels. But she worked hard as an artist and Winnie didn't understand, even after showing her sister her praise in the international newspaper, that she was just as important as they were.

Harper's mind seemed to freeze up when it occurred to her what it was that Winnie wanted. There wasn't any way that she expected her to.... Surely she didn't mean for her to sleep with her husband and get pregnant. Just so they could have this perfect little being to make in an image just like them. No, her mind told her, that couldn't be what they wanted.

"Pay me for what? To find you a child?" Harper was positive that she was misunderstanding them. Or at least she hoped she was. When Winnie accused her of being obtuse, Harper had had enough. "Perhaps you can explain this to me. Tell me what it is you want to pay me to do for you. Not that

I'm going to do it, mind you, but you can explain it."

"Of course you're going to do it, Harper. You will because this is what I want. We want you to carry our child for us. Like I said, it's not like you have anything else to do with your time." Harper had just stared at them. "You will have to have better living arrangements, starting now, of course. Your house is nice enough, but it's in a terrible neighborhood. And we'll ensure that you have the best of care when you finally get pregnant. Eat better too. No more coffee for you. I have a list of things that you're going to have to give up, and I've ordered you some exercise equipment that you'll use on this schedule that I've—"

"Wait. I'm not going to have your child. I mean, thanks, but no thanks. I have things I want to do for myself, and being your surrogate isn't going to happen. There is no way I'm going to give up the next year of my life for you to have a kid, Winnie. No way. You can't possibly be serious about this." Winnie asked her what she was talking about, she'd explained it all and Harper would do it. As if her having their child was a done deal. "I'm not going to do this, Winnie. I have no idea why you'd think I'd even consider this. I have things to do as well. I just don't understand why you'd even think...? You know what, I don't fucking care. No, I'm not going to do this for you. You want a child, then you carry it. Or go find some other idiot to do it for you."

"I can't have a child." She had been moving to the door and her sister's words stopped her. "I can't have children. Not with the way my life is going right now. I'm on top of the world, Harper. I thought you'd be happy for me...for Jake and me. I don't understand why you'd not think that you're going to do this for us. We'd make sure you have care and money. Is that what this is all about? You need more money?"

"No, I have money. Enough for me. But there isn't enough cash in the world for me to get with your idiotic idea. You don't even like me." Winnie didn't even try and deny it, she only shrugged. "Why, Winnie? Why are you doing this? You can't want a baby in your home to mess things up for you. Do you have any idea how much work it is going to be?"

"Yes. I've done research. And I don't know what you're so upset about. I practically raised you." Harper just laughed. "Well, I did see that you were put in a good home when Mom died."

"You did at that. And had I not learned a few lessons in protecting myself from Billy Target that lived down the street, I'd be dead by now. So thank you for that." Her sister huffed at her. "I'm not going to do it, Winnie. Go and find someone else to carry your child."

As far as she was concerned the matter was closed. Winnie would either find herself another woman to do this for her or she'd do it herself. Then five days later, when she'd been coming out of her home to go to the grocery, Harper had been hit from behind and taken someplace. A hospital, Harper thought, but she was wrong, so very wrong.

Her sister had set her up. Winnie had decided that she was going to carry her child no matter what Harper felt about the entire thing. Winnie had not only arranged for her to be hurt, but kidnapped, taken to a remote place, and then tested, monitored, and probed for two months until the timing was right for her to carry their child. Then in no time at all, Harper was impregnated with Jake's kid and getting larger with it every day. That had been almost eight months ago.

The knock at the door startled her out of her memories. Harper didn't know anyone here, hadn't ordered any food as yet, and was pretty sure that the guy who had tried to get into her room wouldn't be back. Not to mention, he certainly wouldn't be knocking. Not after what she'd done to him.

Going to the door, she looked through the peephole and wasn't surprised to see that not only was it next to impossible to make the man out, there also wasn't any light outside the door where she could see him.

They're the men I was telling you about. Harper nearly fell back from the door when the fucking dragon, or whatever he was, spoke to her. *Lord Kenton is a doctor, and he can see to you.*

"See to me? What does that mean? In the event you've not noticed when raping my mind, I'm not really into trusting a doctor right now." He told her that he was a good man. "Yes, I'm sure you might think he is, but I'm still not going to let him in. If it's all the same to you, I've had enough visitors today to last me for the rest of my life." Then she heard laughter on the other side of the door.

"Miss Bailey? My name is Kenton McCade. I'm a doctor. My brother, Grady, is here with me. We've been told you've been hurt, and we've come a long way to see if we can help you." She looked at her arm that was still bleeding. "I can smell it, the blood. And it smells like you've lost a lot of it. Can you please let us in? Your neighbors are starting to come out to look at us."

She leaned against the door. Harper was exhausted, hungry, and hurting. And here was a man telling her that she was bleeding to death. Then what he said occurred to her.

"Okay, I might not be as smart as most people, but how the hell can you smell when someone has lost a lot of blood?" When the man on the other side of the door laughed, she wasn't encouraged, nor impressed. "Also, how the hell do I know you are what you say you are? For all I know, you could be some nutball that wants to come in here and have sex with a very fat woman."

If you would only open the door, they can help you. She didn't want to...Harper didn't want a damned thing to do with these people and their jewelry. The dragon had told her over and over that she needed to wear the torque so that he could keep her safe. And now that she had the stupid thing on her arm, she felt like there was more shit going on than before. Harper just wanted things back the way they'd been before all this.

Leaning against the door, she tried to stop the tears that seemed to be falling all the time. Harper wanted someone to help her, to hold her when she was emotional and make sure that she had a safe life. But there wasn't anyone there for her, all because of her fucking sister. And now here she was, with two men outside her door trying to help. She wasn't sure there was enough help in the world to get her out of this one.

Opening the door was one of the hardest things she had ever done. Standing there, seeing the two of them for the first time, she wondered what the fuck they were feeding people in Ohio. These guys, like the one that had hurt her, were as big as a fucking house.

"I'm not sure about this." The man with the big bag nodded and moved into the room with her. The other man, younger by a few years, she'd bet, just stood there. When the baby kicked her, she put her hand over her belly and watched his face as he stared at her. "My sister's kid."

"Yeah? How does that work?" She told him she'd been tricked into being a surrogate for her. "Tricked? I'm assuming that there is a story there, but if you don't mind, we'd like to get you fixed up first. Also, do you know if there is a place here that might bring food? We kind of left in a hurry."

"Yes. But I'd not recommend it. The last time I had pizza delivered, the guy thought his tip should be me on my back.

I'm not into forced sex any more than I am forced pregnancies."
He grinned at her and she wondered if he knew how sexy that
was. "You should know that I don't charm easily. I've been
screwed over enough for several lifetimes."

"I won't hurt you." For some weird reason she believed
him. "Kenton and I are the dragons you've been told about.
I'm sure that the dragon—Caelin is his name, in the event
that he didn't tell you—has been telling you how we're all
connected, correct?"

"Yes. But that doesn't mean much to me." She moved out
of his way when he asked to come in. Grabbing the wall to
keep herself from falling, she squeaked when he picked her
up in his arms. "Good heavens, put me down. I must weigh
a ton."

"Actually, you're very light. I thought you'd be heavier."
She wasn't sure if he'd just insulted her or not, but decided to
let it go for now. "Now, I'm going to hold you while Kenton
takes care of your cut. Then you're going to tell us about this
pizza guy. He and I need to have a little conversation. That is
no way to treat a lady, and he'll soon learn that lesson when
I find him."

It was too much. Harper wasn't sure how this hormone
thing was supposed to work, but at the smallest thing, she'd
be a mess. Now was no different. As she sobbed out her story
to the two of them, Kenton pulled out a little vial of something
and she felt a needle pinch in her arm. He was telling her she
was going to be fine now even as she drifted off.

Harper wanted to tell him she'd not been fine in a long
time, but she was too fuzzy to make her mouth work. Even
as she snuggled up to the man who held her, she had the
strangest feeling that she was in more trouble than she'd been
before all this.

CHAPTER 2

Grady turned in his seat so that he could see her in the back. While she was buckled in, a pillow behind her head, he still worried about her being sore when she woke up. He looked over at Kenton when he said his name.

"Do you know what she meant about being tricked into being a surrogate? I mean, has dragon told you?" Grady said that he'd been quiet since they'd gotten to the hotel. "Yeah, to me as well. I thought he'd at least tell us something, but I can't get him to answer me."

Kenton had cut away her sleeve when he'd stitched her up. The dragons on her upper arm had startled Grady, but when he touched them with his finger, he knew that it was the torque that Caelin had told them about. And without a doubt, she was his mate. Grady had been trying to get Caelin to tell him why she wasn't just wearing them but they were a part of her. No answer. Then suddenly he spoke.

I've been researching it, the reason why she doesn't wear them but they have moved into her flesh. Grady told Kenton what the dragon had been doing and perhaps had an answer. *They aren't a part of the original set. I can only surmise that because of that, they do not act like the other pieces of the jewelry. So as soon as she put it on her arm, it became a part of her. I did as well.*

31

"A part of her how?" Caelin said that it was a sigil for her, while the others wore their jewelry. "Will I be marked like this as well?"

I know not, my lord. I have only guessed at this. There is nothing in my memories that say this should happen. There was, at one time, a woman who wore the piece for a spell, but she was killed not long after she put them to her skin. I can only think that as Harper is your mate, you will be marked as well. He tried to think what came with the torques. When nothing came to him, he asked. *The muscles in your legs and arms will be greatly increased. Hands and feet as well, but you'll be able to notice it more in your larger muscles. I believe that your mate has used these powers to keep herself safe for you. The man who had come to kill her was pushed away by her new strength.*

Grady looked at his hand and tried to see a difference. There wasn't any as far as he could see, but he'd not mated with her as yet, so maybe that was why. He looked over at Kenton when he asked him if he thought he could fly or not.

"Do you want me to shift right here and figure that out?" Kenton told him he was tired and wanted a distraction. "I'm sure that if I became a dragon right now, you'd have that and more. Besides, don't I have to have sex with her or something to make that happen?"

"You will not be having sex with me." He turned and looked at Harper. "Where are we going? And why the hell are you talking about sex with me?"

"Back home, to where my family can help you." She told him he didn't need any help. "Oh? And how have you been faring so far on your own? Caelin said that you've been hurt several times over the last few weeks. Shot at as well. That working out for you?"

"You're a prick, anyone ever tell you that before?" He

pretended to think about it and then nodded at her. "Funny. I want you to take me back to my hotel and leave me alone. While I appreciate you fixing me up, I'm not going to bother you guys anymore. Especially since I'm sure you think I'm an easy lay because I'm knocked up."

"You said that, how your sister tricked you. Would you mind explaining that? I, for one would like to know how you get a surrogate that way." He was sure she wasn't going to answer him, so he decided to have a little fun with her. "Did she drug you then implant someone's seed in you?"

"Her husband's." He watched her face, and knew that even though he'd been kidding with her, he'd hit it right on the head. "She asked me to have her child for her...well, she didn't ask; Winnie never asks for anything, but demands. But she set everything up for me, including a schedule for a treadmill that she had delivered to my house. Told me that I didn't have a life to mess up by getting pregnant for her and carrying this child, so why would I turn her down for something so stupid? She isn't a nice person, in the event you didn't get that just now. Winnie even went so far as to tell me that she couldn't have children messing up her perfect body. What bullshit. Not that I fell for it, but I was still caught up in her little scheme. So a few days after I left, telling her that there wasn't any way on this earth I was going to do this, she had me hit over the head, taken to some remote place, and poked and prodded until I was ripe. Fuck, I hate her right now."

Grady told her he was sorry. When she waved him off, he wanted to crawl over the seat and go back and hold her. She looked so sad at the moment, and beaten. Grady wondered what sort of person did this to their own flesh and blood.

"They took me to this clinic for two months. Well, that's

not quite right. It was a big metal building that had a blocked off section where I was watched, all the fucking time. And when I fought them, they'd shoot a dart at me from this little window and knock me out. Every day someone would come in and take my temperature and blood. They served these meals that only an insane person would want to eat, and measured my pee. Who the fuck measures pee when they don't have to? Anyway, it wasn't until the second week, when my sister came to see me, that I finally had a clue as to what they were doing."

Grady watched her face. She was upset, yes, but he was sure it was more than that. Betrayal too. She'd been betrayed by the one person that should have been there for her. Grady didn't have any idea what he'd do without one or all of his brothers. Before he could offer her any kind of sympathy, something he was sure she'd not want, she spoke again.

"Winnie said that it wasn't as if anyone would miss me if I didn't show up for my morning cereal. She had taken care of my mail, and had someone water my plants. Then she told me that I should have thanked her when she'd gone out of her way to make things better for me. Bitch. And on top of that, she called me a deadbeat." She laughed bitterly. "Winnie doesn't like being told no, I guess."

"I'm so sorry. No one should have been treated that way. And the fact that she did this regardless of your feelings shows just what sort of person she is." Harper looked at him, and he could see that she was more hurt than she was saying to them. "We'll get through his, Harper, I promise you we will."

"When I first woke up, I thought that I'd contracted this rare disease or something like that. Something that would spread all over the world, and they were using me to make a serum or something. Never in a million years would I have thought that she'd go this far. That was when I found out that they were testing me to find out when I'd be ovulating. As soon as I hit peak time, or whatever it's called, I was put under by something in my food and this happened. I woke up tied to the bed then, monitors all over my body." He asked if she was all right now. "I suppose so. If you discount the fact that I'm carrying a child that I neither wanted nor had much in the way of say in. It's like they raped me. You know what I mean? Did this to me without permission. And Winnie is responsible."

"I would have thought they'd keep you there until you were to term." Grady wanted to hit Kenton when he spoke. "I'm sorry. That was callous of me, but I would like to know why they let you out. I'm assuming that your sister had a change of heart? Or did she get pregnant?"

"Oh, she had a change of heart all right. When she found out she was carrying her husband's child about three months into this shit, she had a lot of them. First of all, she didn't want it or the one that she'd paid so much to have planted in me. And her husband, he was pissed off because—and this is a quote—he 'did not want to deal with it.' I haven't any idea what they might have done when the baby was actually theirs. Dealing with it, as he said, would have been a lot harder. So she told me that I had ten days to come to an arrangement with being pregnant. It took me a bit longer than it should have to realize that she wanted me to abort the baby. I guess that was her way of dealing with it." Harper looked at him as she continued. "I've not spoken to her since I got the first registered letter from her attorney. She had the nerve to send me a bill for what she did as well. All one hundred and forty grand of it. As if I had some say in any of this. Telling me that since she no longer had a use for the child, and since I wasn't going to get rid of it, that I needed to sign off on paperwork that said that it wasn't her husband's, and that I'd never try and get anything from them for as long as the child was alive. Also, I was to never tell anyone what happened. She didn't want it to get around that they'd had a change of heart concerning a baby. What sort of person does that? I mean, who would tell me to get an abortion after all they'd done to get me this way? Christ, I really didn't like her before. I positively hate her now."

"Do you want to keep the child now?" Instead of answering him, she looked out the window. "Harper, is she trying to hurt you about the money and the child?"

"She hurt me the moment she kidnapped me." He nodded, but knew that she'd not seen him. "I'm not sure where you guys are taking me, but if you could just pull over, I'd really like to get out. I really appreciate you helping me, but this is not your problem. As nice as you've been to me, I don't want her dragging you down as well."

Grady said nothing to her. She was crying again and his heart hurt for her. Reaching out to Dalton, he told him what he'd been able to gather from her and asked him to see what else he could find. He'd hit on the names right away.

Says here that Winnifred and Jake Patrick have filed a judgment against your mate. It doesn't say much, only that she needs to pay them for services rendered. Just a hair under a hundred and forty grand, it looks like. And they're pushing it pretty hard to recoup their losses, as they're calling it. There is also another article that I'm looking at that says the couple had been married for four years. Both seem to have very successful careers and have had some pretty lavish parties. Jake was up for partner in his firm, and Winnie, as she goes by, is on the cover of a lot of magazines and – His brother was laughing when he started talking again. *Grady, your mate is pretty famous herself. More so than her sister, I think. She is an artist. Her work is right up there with Jorden's. Accolades from all over the world for her work, which can be seen in a few galleries both here and around the world.*

What sort of media does she use? Dalton told him she was a potter. *I wonder if Jorden knows her or her work. But that doesn't negate the fact that she's been hurt now. Harper just told us how her sister kidnapped and then impregnated her with Jake's child. Then after they figured out that they didn't want the baby, they tried unsuccessfully to get her to abort it. She mentioned, too, that they want her to sign something that says that she'll not tell anyone whose kid it is. This is really bad, Dalton. Really bad.*

He looked back at her and wondered if her sister knew anything about her, and from the sounds of it, he doubted it. Dragon took that moment to tell him about the conversation that had transpired between Winnie and Harper just before she found the torque.

Harper had called her sister to ask about the lawsuit just after she was released from the hospital and given notice of the billing. She asked her what on earth she would owe money for. I had to search her mind to find out what that might be. Winnie told her that she wanted her money back, and Harper pointed out to her that she didn't want to carry her child in the first place, and that she should be paying her, not the other way around. Winnie pointed out that she'd told her to get rid of the child, but she hadn't. I don't care for this woman. Her sister is not a nice person. Grady told him that he didn't think so either. *The child belongs to Winnie's husband; they are all aware of that. But when Winnie wished her sister to kill the child, she told her she'd never do that. She doesn't want Harper to try to get money from them later in the form of blackmail, her sister told her. She thinks that the child would be better off dead than with Harper, who Winnie thinks is a person without any kind of moral code of conduct.*

Yet here she is trying to not only get her sister to kill the child off, but to pay her back for actions that she had no say in. She's a real peach, this Winnie person is. And I cannot wait to meet her face to face. I don't think she's going to like me any better than she does Harper.

Grady asked Caelin and Dalton to keep looking for information. In the meantime, he thought that she'd be better off if no one, her sister included, knew where she'd gone. Grady asked Kenton how much longer before they were home.

"Half an hour." Grady nodded and looked back at Harper, who was sleeping. "When we get there, where am I taking her? I need to let Mom know."

"My house." He wasn't sure that was a good idea or not, but he figured that if she didn't like it there, she could go with his mom. But he was going to try his very best to get her to stay with him. He was worried for her health and that of her baby. Not that he thought she'd harm it, but he was worried about all the undue stress. He asked Kenton about it.

"She looks to be in her last trimester, which puts her close to term." Grady nodded. "Her ankles are swollen, I noticed, and she's more than likely dehydrated. When you get her home, have her drink plenty of water or juice, and she'll need to put her feet up higher than her nose. Toes to nose."

"I remember that. Yes, I'll try. What else should I do to make her more comfortable?" Kenton looked at him, then back at the road. "Whatever you're thinking, I want to know."

"Grady, we don't know if someone is chasing her yet. Whether the pizza guy was with the dragon killers, or if her sister is going to come here. Nor do we know about this guy who came after her other than he left. Why? Where did he come from, and where is he now? We need a plan." He agreed, but told Kenton he was too tired to think right now. "So am I. But we have to protect her more than the others. With the baby coming, she's going to be an easy target for whoever is after her."

He'd thought of that too. When they came for her, and he had no doubt that someone would, they'd get her by way of the child. Because while he didn't know her well, he was sure that she would do nothing to harm that unborn child. It was his child now, as far as he was concerned, and no one, not any of them, was going to hurt either of them.

As soon as they pulled up in front of his house, she woke. He wasn't sure of her reaction to the place…it was sort of dark out and he could only see how stiff she was. Picking her up against her protests, Grady carried her into the house and up to the guest room. He laid her on the bed and waited for the fireworks. And he was sure there would be some.

~~~

"What the fuck do you think you're doing?" He said that he was making sure she was comfortable. "I'm not, in the event that you didn't notice. Do you have any idea how cumbersome I am? How fat I feel? Comfort has long since become a thing of the past for me."

"No, I have no idea. What I can tell you is that I think you're pretty. And not fat at all, but glowing with the fact that you're with child. No, I'd say that you're very beautiful." She wasn't sure what to say to that. He smiled at her and she wanted to hit him. But for reasons that she couldn't put her finger on at the moment, she was also charmed by him. Standing up and holding onto the bedpost, she was surprised when he put his hand out for her to hold. It was warm and comforting to be taken care of, even for a little while. "After you've rested a bit, if you like you can shower. There are clean towels in the bathroom there. And an extra blanket in the chest at the end of the bed. I don't know if you noticed or not back at the hotel, but we gathered your things and brought them with us. Also, I've asked Rachel to press or wash them up if they need it. For now there is clean clothing I can lend you. They'll be huge on you, but they'll serve to keep you dressed."

The door behind him opened and a tall woman walked in with a tray. She was followed by an equally tall man with a stack of something…she thought it was more towels, but it turned out to be a robe. She took it from him when he handed it to her. She watched them fuss around the room as Grady continued.

"This is Rachel, our housekeeper, and her husband, Walker. They will keep you safe when I'm not here. Unless you want to come with me to the shop." Harper nodded. "All right then. I'm going to go down and have some breakfast, then I'll see what we can do about getting you some clothing. If you're hungry, I'll wait for you to eat. That'll give Rachel time to whip us up something besides cereal."

"I'd like a shower first, if you don't mind." He pointed to the door again where he'd said the towels were. "I don't know what's going on here, but I don't like being in the dark. I also don't know why you've brought me here and are caring for me like this. I think I deserve an answer to at least that."

"I agree. You do deserve answers. But I don't have a lot of them right now, not on all of this. However, if you want to know something else, ask me. If I know the answer, I'll give it to you. If I don't, then we'll find it together. I would like the same from you." She nodded at him again. "Good. There are any number of people that are around working on the house. Either Walker or Rachel can tell you if you can trust them."

"Can I trust you?" He told her with her life. And again, for some reason she believed him. "You said that they'd tell me who I can trust. How many people do you know that you don't trust?"

"Sadly, a great many. My mother is here now. She's pushy and will tell you to rest a great deal. But she'd never harm you. Not for any reason. My sister-in-law, Emma, is with her, and she is scary bossy, but one of the nicest people you'll meet. Jasmine is around, my other sister-in-law, but not close at the moment. You'll meet the rest of my family soon...tonight, I think." He grinned at her when he took the robe and led her to the bathroom. "Take a long hot shower, and when you're finished, I'll have Rachel help you with the dressing on your arm. Kenton said you could get it wet, but to change it as soon as you were done. Do you need anything?"

"Yes. Answers." He nodded this time. "I don't understand you. Why are you being so nice to me? Is it because of the dragon and the stories he told me?"

"Did he tell you what you are to me?" She told him that he had, but she didn't believe it. "That's fair. I'm to understand that you know a couple of shifters...a wolf and cat."

"Yes. They're friends...they were friends of mine." He asked her what had happened to them. She wanted to tell him, but didn't. Her mind was still trying to wrap around their deaths and how they'd been killed. "I'd like a shower now, please."

"Of course. Take your time and when you're finished, we'll have some breakfast together and go to my store. It opens in two weeks, and I have a lot of work to be done yet. It'll be nice to have the company."

She was turning on the water to the large stall when a knock sounded at the door. Harper wasn't sure who it could be so she asked without opening it. The laughter on the other side was female, so she opened it to see.

"Hi. I'm Emma McCade. You must be Harper." Harper said she was. "Good. It would just be silly to find someone else in this room, don't you think? Anyway. I have some things for you to wear after you're done. Your clothing is being washed right now, so here you go."

There was a man's shirt, as well as a pair of pants that looked like they were too small. But upon closer inspection, she realized they were actually both maternity things. Holding them close to her, she asked where they had come from.

"There's a pack of wolves on the land that are very good friends of ours. Two of the women are breeding right now. Pregnant. Anyway, they brought them over when Kenton asked. You met him, he's my husband." Harper asked her if he was the doctor. "Yes, that's him. And if you don't mind, he'd like for you to go by his office so he can check you over as soon as you can manage it. Nothing untoward, but he wants to make sure that the tumble with the guy that rushed you didn't hurt either of you."

"All right. That man who came with the gun, do you know why he was after me?" Emma told her it was because of the dragons. "So I should expect more of them, someone to come and try to take me from this place too?"

"Yes. You can expect them to come, but they're not going to get you to go anywhere. Not now that you're with family." Harper asked her why she was counted as family. "Because for as much as you don't want to believe it, we are. The moment that you came here—even before, I guess—we were already here to help protect you, and the babe you carry."

"My sister and her husband, do you count them as people that you'd protect me from?" Emma smiled and told her from anyone that tried to harm her, no matter who or what. "I don't understand you people. You know nothing about me. I could be as bad as Winnie."

"From what I've heard, no one is as bad as Winnie except maybe her husband. Dalton, another McCade brother, is a cop, and he's looking into things for you about them. Lewis and I, we'll keep you well fed and happy that way. Jasmine is Jorden's wife…she owns and operates an antique store. She's working today or would be here. They have a son, Gavin, who is extremely smart and one of the politest kids you'll ever meet. Vance, he's…. Well, Vance is a person that you can trust with your life, but he's a little intense. The rest of the family you've met. Oh, and Aisha, their mom. She's wonderful. You'll love her to pieces."

Harper was overwhelmed and said that to Emma. Nodding as if she understood completely, Emma told her to take a nice shower and they'd talk more. Also, Emma said they'd figure out where Winnie and her husband were to keep tabs on them.

After closing the door again, Harper adjusted the water to a nice temp and stripped down. The bruises on her arms were already turning dark. Ignoring them, she looked at the two dragons on her bicep. And she thought of how, just because they were there, she'd been able to deal with the man who had come for her.

Yesterday she'd ordered a pizza. Not that big of a deal, but she was craving one in the worst kind of way. She knew that she'd have heartburn and be a little sick after, but she needed it…like breathing. After finding a place that would deliver to the small hotel, she went to her luggage to find the notes on pieces of pottery that she wanted to design if she ever got out of this mess.

43

Just a short ten minutes after she'd gotten her dinner and had to run the boy off, there was a knock at her door again. Standing as she was eating the second piece of the worst pizza she'd ever eaten, the door exploded open. A kid no older than some of the ones she'd seen at the high school where she taught a few days a week came in with a gun.

"Come with me and bring your jewelry." Shaking her head, she reached for anything to protect herself with. "I didn't ask you, I said to come with me. We know that you have a piece of it and that you brought it with you, so get it. I don't have time for you to be shitting around on this. Come on."

The torque touched her fingers as she was reaching for something to hit him with, and she was calmed by the simple act. The voice in her head, the dragon, told her to slip it on and he'd help her. The moment that she wrapped it around her wrist, thinking that had to be what he meant, she felt empowered. Not only that, but she knew just what she had to do to save herself and her child. But the young kid, the gun toting boy, seemed pissed when he saw that she'd put it on.

"Well fuck, lady. You sure as shit screwed this up for me, didn't you?" She asked him what he meant, the gun pointed at her head now. "I was supposed to get the jewels then kill you so that you'd not be able to get to the family. I didn't think you'd actually put it on. Damn it all to fuck and back. Now I have to cut off your fucking arm. But I will get it no matter what it takes, just like I was told."

When he came at her, she put out her hand to stop him, like that would have done her a bit of good. The surge of power that ran up her arm to her fist astounded her, and the kid, apparently, because he stopped moving toward her and actually took a step in retreat. But he went flying back when she pushed her hand at him, the knowledge that it would get rid of him pounding at her head.

She was glad then that the door had been left open, or he might have broken it down and she'd have no way of closing herself in while she thought. The furniture hadn't done as well. It looked as if it had been smashed, like a large fist had pounded it to splinters. Sitting down hard on the bed, she felt drained and sick to her stomach. The dragon spoke to her then.

They're coming. She asked him who. *The McCades. They're on their way to help you. Stay in the room and they'll be here soon. You must be safe.*

"I don't need help. What the fuck was that? That unholy power that came out of my hand? And how the hell did I know how to use it?" He didn't answer her. "For days now all you've done is talk, talk, talk. And now you shut up? What's going on?"

That man, he tried to kill you. The second one. You did well to rid yourself of him. She told him no shit. *You are unharmed then? The babe, he's all right?*

"Yes. Do you know what that was about? He said that he was going to cut my arms off. Why? And don't think I didn't notice that you didn't answer me about the power, either." He told her because of the jewelry that she wore. "You mean the one that you told me to put on? The same jewelry that you said would keep me safe? That jewelry? For fuck sake, are you trying to get me killed?"

He started to explain things to her, to tell her what was going on. But she told him to shut up. To leave her alone. He begged her over the next hour to talk to him, but she shut him out. Her mind hadn't really shut down, but it was like it was dealing with too much and turned to things that were easier

45

to see. Like designs for pottery she wanted to make. What she was going to get to eat when she was hungry.

But no matter what she thought of, the fact that she had no idea how she'd done that kept coming back. As for the dragon, he'd nearly gotten her killed and she was done with him. And now here she was, in a stranger's house, about to put on someone else's clothing, and she was no closer to figuring this shit out than she'd been before. Plus, her sister was still after her.

The water felt good running over her body. She had been on the run for a few weeks now, ever since her sister had put out a warrant for her arrest and the dragon had told her to take the jewelry to Ohio. So taking a long hot shower hadn't been an option. Not when she had to listen for every little sound. Be aware of every voice she heard, in her head and surrounding her.

Harper could have paid her sister off, she supposed, but she didn't think any of this was her doing and thought that Winnie should be paying her. Harper was nearly nine months pregnant and she'd not even had sex with the guy. Laughing, she washed up her body and hair, and finished her bath thinking that sleeping with Jake would be the last thing on her mind, even before all this shit. It was time to talk to the McCades, she supposed, and figure out what the hell was going on with them.

The outfit was beautiful, and it fit over her growing frame very nicely. The blue of the top was what she might have picked out for herself; the cut of it, like a man's dress shirt, felt good on her. Even the pants were a soft stretchy like cloth that fit over her legs and belly like a glove. And for the first time in a while, her feet weren't aching from being too swollen.

The underthings, a bra that was the same violet color as

the panties, also fit. They were new with the tags still on them, so she wasn't worried about pulling them on. She moved out into the bedroom to find an elderly lady sitting on the chair by the fireplace. Her smile was reassuring and looked just like Grady's, only a softer version.

"Don't be alarmed. I'm Grady's mom, Aisha." Harper sat on the bed and put her feet up when the woman pushed a stool to her. "Kenton guesses that you're about in your last month. He also noticed that your ankles are swollen. He'd like to check you out soon."

"His wife, Emma, told me that. Why?" Aisha asked her what she meant. "Why do you care that I have fat ankles and if I'm close to term? I am, by the way. About three weeks to go. But to be honest, I've not had a lot of prenatal care, other than what I can find on the Internet. I've been running for a couple of months now, just to keep one step ahead of Winnie and this mad group of people after me for some jewelry. My sister wants my money, and I have this annoying dragon pestering me about coming here."

"I heard about that. Dreadful girl. She needs to be whipped." Harper smiled. She loved this woman already. "I'm to tell you two things. First, however, you are so lovely, and Grady was right, you are glowing with your baby. But the two things. Jorden and Jasmine, my son and his wife, will be around today to see you—"

"Jorden McCade?" She nodded. "You're Jorden McCade's mother? The famous guy who paints? You're related to him? And he's...are you kidding me? You're related to Jorden McCade?"

"Yes. He's my son. You know his work?" Harper was having a very bad fangirl moment, but managed to nod. "Would you like to meet him?"

"Yes. When?" Aisha told her he was in the kitchen now. "Here? In this kitchen? Well hell, what are we waiting for? Jorden McCade is in the house, and I'm going to meet him."

CHAPTER 3

Grady was having a hard time not laughing at his brother. Jorden, he knew, was famous, but it was funny watching him deal with Harper. Grady wasn't sure who was more impressed, nor which of them was doing better at not fawning all over the other. Both of them seemed to be great fans of the other's work. He cleared his throat when he noticed the time.

"I have to get to work. I'm sorry, but I really do need to get the product on the shelves or I won't be opening on time." Jorden said they were there to help out. "Good. I can use it. Gavin said he'd come by as well when he was finished with his homework."

"If you guys don't mind, I'll take Harper to see Kenton. He's sort of cleared his morning to have her checked out." Grady wanted to be there with her, but Jasmine told him that this first time, it should be only the two of them. "That way if there are any problems, which I'm doubting there are, you won't freak out."

"I do not freak out." Jorden pointed out the truck and the over ordering. Then he explained what had happened to Harper. "That wasn't my fault. I have too much inventory and the bill is too low."

"It's yours." They all turned to Harper. "I mean, it could

49

be different in Ohio, but if the inventory sheet said what you were to get and the prices that you were quoted, then it's yours at that price. Especially if you called them."

"Several times. So did the driver. They told us both that they don't makes mistakes." Harper nodded. "I'm having the family attorney look into that and some other things. I don't think this is a scam, but you never know."

After Harper left with Emma and Jasmine, Jorden sat down with him. Grady really wanted to get to the shop, but he had a feeling that Jorden wanted something. When he sat down with his brother, Jorden handed him a thick envelope. Grady asked him what it was, not opening it as yet.

"You remember when I told you some time back about the inventory in the houses?" He nodded. "Okay, well, once all of you told us what you wanted to get rid of, we put it in the shop. Jasmine kept track of all the pieces, and when she sold them off, put the money for them aside. To give to the person who owned it. This is your part of the sales."

"I don't want this." Jorden said he figured he'd say that. "No, I'm serious. Emma sold me this house cheap, and Jasmine did me a huge favor by taking the stuff rather than giving it to the dump. The only way I was able to afford something this nice is because of the two of them. If that's money, which I'm assuming it is, then you tell her to use it for evil or something."

"I have an idea on what to use it for. So you know, the others turned down the money as well. But I had to tell you about it, you know that?" Grady said he did. "What if we take this money—and I will admit, it's a lot more than I thought it would be—but what if we used the money toward the shelter that Emma was talking about? You know, the place they can come in and take a shower or get a hot meal. Not a place to sleep yet. That requires a great deal more in the way of regulations than I know how to get around right now, and Douglas has his hands full with the other things we have going. So for now, I'd like to use it to hire more people to get everything done."

"You mean just use it to get the building up to code? How would that work exactly? I mean, that's a lot of money going in without any return. Not that I care one way or the other, but it won't sustain itself for long if we don't have some sort of payback, right?" Jorden nodded and handed him a sheet of paper. It had been handwritten for the most part, things marked out and others added in different handwriting. "The others are onboard with this? I like some of these ideas; others.... Well, I know that this is just the beginning, but there are a couple on here that I think we can do right now. Such as getting the hot water turned on, as well as towels."

"Yes. Very much so. You're the last one I had to talk to. And if you know where to call to get towels cheap, and also a washer and dryer, I'd appreciate your help on that as well." Grady read over the rest of the notes as Jorden continued. "I was going to ask you yesterday, but I got sidetracked. Again."

He liked what was written. The people would pay for their items by helping out around the building. Sweeping up. Taking out the trash. There was going to be a place for them to take a shower, and Kenton had volunteered his time in a makeshift clinic as well. Gavin had written that computers could be added at some point to help with skill sets. There was even an addition that his mom had written in for crafts, something that they could do to sell in one of the local shops when they were opened.

"I'm in." Jorden grinned at him. "I haven't any idea what I can do to help out, but you can count on me for more than just the towels and a washer and dryer. Maybe I can fix up some old computers for them, like Gavin suggested, and bring them in. Or, I don't know, teach some of them how to use the ones you might already have."

"We don't have any, and I was hoping that we could count on you for that part. This is great. I think this money will go a long way in not just getting this set up, but to keep it going for a while as well." He stood up, then stopped as he made his way to the door. "By the way, I've heard through the grapevine that Doug Norton and Norton Computers is going under. And I think it was because they lost the contract with the university. I guess that was a big money maker for him."

"Yes, it was. I got a call from the university this morning when I got home. Apparently, they figured out that I wasn't working for Norton any longer and cut ties with him. Mr. Shipley, the guy that runs the department, said that Doug was telling him that I was on vacation, and that as soon as I returned he'd send me right over." There was more to the conversation than that, but Grady didn't tell Jorden. But he'd bet anything his brother knew. "I'm going to help them out. I don't know if I want to sign a contract yet, but they've asked me to come in and fix a few things for them. Also, just between us, they've asked me to teach a few classes as well. Some adult learning things. I haven't said yes yet, but I'm thinking about it. It would only be a couple of nights a week, and I'd get benefits. I could take some classes there as well, I was told."

"You should do it, Grady. You're very good at computers. Not to mention, you can really make a difference in someone's life if they learn to use a computer when they've never done it before. One more thing. You should know that Harper's sister knows she's here. Not with you, but in the area. Apparently there was a thing in the paper about the break-in at the hotel and that she was in town. Harper was mentioned as someone that had been hurt. I'd keep her close if I were you." Grady said that was the plan he had as well. "Douglas said that you've got him looking into things for her about the pregnancy, as well as how it had happened."

"Yes. He's already found two of the people that worked at this clinic where she was taken. They treated her well for the most part, but it was still against her will. I guess he's trying to get the video of her stay there as well, in the event that this goes to court." Jorden nodded. "I have a favor to ask you, too. I don't have any idea of what sort of things Harper needs to work in what she does, but do you still have that wheel around? I'd like to buy it from you if you want to get rid of it."

"I have it set up in my studio, as a matter of fact. Why don't you bring her by after her appointment with Kenton, and we can see what else she needs? Whatever it is, I'm sure that I can find it for her. There is even a kiln there should she want to use it until we can get her something bigger and better. Christ, Grady, do you have any idea how famous your mate is?" He said that he'd not had the chance to look yet. "Trust me when I tell you, her name brings people from all over to buy her pieces. I was actually thinking of asking her to share my studio with me. And a gallery if I open one."

"I think that she was going to ask you the same thing, if she could work there with you. I don't know about the gallery part; you'll have to work that out with her, but she's excited to be working with the famous Jorden McCade." Grady laughed when his brother's face turned a nice shade of pink. "I tell you, watching the two of you fall all over each other is hilarious."

After Jorden left, Grady made his way to the shop, Dragon Computers, a name that he'd been thinking of for his shop since he'd worked for his previous employer. It was going to be great, he knew it, if he ever got the thing opened. As he turned on lights he couldn't help but be both proud of his place and terrified at the same time.

Just as he was locking up behind him, his mom knocked on the door. "I came to help you out." He let her in, knowing that there was something else to this. It was Wednesday, and he knew that she had her garden club on Wednesday mornings. "I even brought some cookies from Emma to eat. Oh, and her and Lewis are having another cook-off this weekend. I think the main ingredient is pork. I cannot wait."

When he handed her a box knife and she just stared at it, he took it from her and told her to sit. She did so without question, and he was nervous. His mom had something on her mind, and he wasn't sure he could help her with whatever it was.

"I don't know how to be a grandma." He just looked at her, not sure what she meant. "I mean, Gavin, he makes it so easy. I think of us more as co-conspirators than grandma to grandson. He's such a joy to be around. But he's already past the stage of coming to me when his mom upsets him, or even Jorden. But a baby, that's a whole different ball of wax. I don't even know what to do with one anymore."

"I'm pretty sure that Gavin comes to you more often than you're saying. I know for a fact that the two of you are working on the charity thing like it's your job." She said that they were going to make so much money at this thing. "I agree. And he loves you so much."

"And I love him as well. But there will be newborns coming soon. Much sooner than I had thought. And while I'm thrilled beyond words, I'm just as scared of messing up." She looked at him and he could see her fear. "What if I don't have any idea how to take care of them? What if I don't follow the rules that Harper might have for her son? I've never — "

"Mom. Just calm down." She nodded and got up to pace the room. He watched her for several seconds before he continued. "What sort of rules do you think there will be? And so you know, I haven't had much in the way of time to talk to Harper about her baby. For all I know, she might want to give it up for adoption."

"She will not." He had to laugh but caught himself just in time. "You're not serious, are you? Do you think she'd do that? I mean, I know that she didn't have any say in the little guy being here, but she's not going to just discard him, is she?"

"I don't think so. But as I said, we've not talked about it." His mom nodded, but continued to pace. "What's brought this on? You've been a wonderful grandma to Gavin, and I'm sure that you will be to the rest of the babies born in this family. What's got you all upset like this?"

"There are rules, you know. I've been reading up on them. Like how to put the baby down for a nap." He asked her why that was important. "They are linking things more and more to Sudden Infant Death. Then there is the whole baby powder thing."

"Baby powder?" Her nod was just sad. "Look, Mom. I haven't any idea what you're reading, but I think you did a great job of raising us. But if you want, I'll talk to Harper when she gets back here today. She wants to hang out with me while I work."

"Good. I'll just ask her then. You think that she'll be all right with me taking on the role as grandma? I mean, she might have a grandma of her own that she wants to have the child love. Not that I won't love it too, but she might not feel the same way." She looked at him and Grady hugged her. "Oh Grady, I'm going to fail at this."

"No you're not. You're going to be the best grandma in the world. As for any other grandma, there isn't any. Her mother raised her alone for the most part, and she passed away a while back. Her father is gone as well; I'm still having Douglas look into that, but there isn't anyone else." His mom said that was sad. "Yes, it is. But you have to do double duty now…be a grandma for all the kids. But I have faith in you."

As they moved boxes around, him setting his mom up so that she could unpack some things for the shelves, he went to the area where he was setting up the computers he was going to sell. He was debating on whether he should pass on his great deal or try and sell them as if he paid full price when someone knocked at his door. At this rate, he thought, he'd be lucky to open in three months. He went to the door to ask whoever it was to either come in and help or go away. But he paused at the door when he saw the woman there.

Grady knew immediately who it was. It seemed as if Winnie Patrick had found him, and she did not look that happy about it. He moved to the door, telling his mom who had come to visit.

~~~

Harper heard the voices even before she and Kenton moved from the back of the computer store to the main floor. She also knew who it was. Her sister's voice could carry across mountains when she was pissed. And she sounded like she was in a real snit too. Before she entered the big showroom where they were, Kenton stopped her.

"Wait to see what she has to say. And you should know that Grady has the room set up with cameras. He did it first to catch people doing crap they shouldn't." She nodded but wasn't so sure about this. "Trust me, honey, he can handle her. Grady is the quiet, I'm-going-to-kick-your-ass type of guy."

"My sister is the carries-a-gun-to-a-knife-fight sort of person. And she's slick too. I've seen her use tears to get what she wanted, and when that didn't work, she hit this guy." Kenton said she'd not do that to Grady. "I'm glad that you think he can handle her, but I'm telling you, she's not a nice person."

"We know that. Dalton is on his way, Jorden is just down the road at his shop should we need him, and Lewis is about fifteen minutes away. We are bringing in reinforcements even as we speak." Harper asked him if he thought that was enough. "I have no idea, but if she fucks with us, I'll turn into my dragon and eat her."

She thought he was kidding. Harper wasn't sure if she wanted him to be or not, but when he turned his back to her and started emptying office supplies onto the shelf, she was a little afraid. Not for Winnie—she'd fucked up and it was her problem—but for Kenton. He might well get sick if he tried to eat Winnie for dinner.

Harper moved to the door, just close enough where she could see in but not be seen. Kenton pretty much ignored the shouting going on while he was setting things on the shelves, like paper and other office supplies. But she had a feeling that not only did he know just what was going on, but he'd be able to repeat every word. She only glanced at him enough to know that he was safe before looking deeper into the room. Harper felt her temper rise when her sister started in on how she had cheated her.

"Harper is going to pay me or I'll take her to court. Right now all I want is what I had to put out and not court costs, but I will get that as well if she doesn't pay me back. After all I've done for her, she does this to me. I set her up with a nice hospital stay. With the best doctors and care. And now she's run off with my property." Grady asked her what property she was talking about. "That kid. All she had to do was get rid of it, and now look…she's run off like she has a right to. I want this settled. It's taking away from my time with work."

"So? Go back to work. No one is stopping you." She watched as Grady turned his back on Winnie, something that she hated more than anything. "Whatever Harper decides, I'm behind her all the way."

"You have nothing to do with this; this is none of your concern. And turn around when I'm speaking to you. I want to see your face when you figure out what sort of person my sister is." Grady didn't turn, but he did say he didn't care what she thought of Harper. "I'm not kidding about this. Turn the fuck around so that I can talk to you. My God, did your mother raise you to be a rude bastard?"

"No, I did not." Harper held her breath when she heard Aisha speak. She'd not even known she was in the room with Grady, much less that she'd say something to her sister. "Nor do I think you were raised to be such a horrid person. My goodness, what did you expect your sister to do when you've threatened her this way? Not to mention kidnapped and abused her. I would have gotten the police involved in this the moment I was set free. The thought of someone like you…. What kind of person are you that you'd do this to your own sister?"

"I'm the best sister in the world, and she had better be saying that to people too. But I did nothing wrong and she knows it. I told her to do this for me and she said no. I don't know what her problem with it was. It's not like she has a thing to do all day." Harper wanted to go out there and hit her sister, but knew that it wouldn't do any good. Her sister was never going to think she was anything but a lazy person.

"It's my husband's child that she carries, and I want it if she's not going to do as I want. Once we decided that we don't want it after all I told her to abort, but she told me no, like it was her choice to make. Then, when no doctor would touch her after she got huge with it, I asked her to sign a waiver that says that she won't tell anyone who the child belongs to. Plus, she was to pay me back all the money we put forth for her to be pampered and taken care of. I'm betting it's the first time in her adult life that she's even gone to a doctor, much less eaten right. Then she ran off, taking that thing with her, and now she refuses to pay me. I've gone to a lot of expense for this, and all I wanted her to do was as I told her. Besides, she shouldn't think of her time cooped up as a hardship, but more of a vacation. And we all know that vacations aren't free."

Grady turned to Winnie then, and Harper was almost afraid to hear what he was going to say. For sure he'd tell her that he agreed with her, that she was lazy and should have signed off on the child. But there wasn't any way that she was going to do either of those things. It wasn't her fucking fault she was pregnant, damn it.

"You think that just because you wanted this baby, and went to all the effort to not only set your sister up but to do this against her will, that it's fine for you to charge her? Not to mention the fact that you held her against her will, raped her to impregnate her with your husband's child, as well as harassed her from the moment you decided that you no longer wanted to deal with it. That's all okay with you?" Winnie said of course. "I see. Well, I guess it really sucks to be you. You're not going to get a thin dime from either of us. The baby will be raised as my son if Harper will allow it, and you should back your skinny ass out of my space before I have you arrested for being a fucking cunt."

59

Harper moved into the room just as her sister slapped Grady. When she drew back again, to no doubt hit him once more, Harper grabbed her arm and twisted it behind her. The screams that came from her sister were not very lady like.

"Let me go, or so help me, Harper, I will take you for everything that you have. Not that you have anything that I want but that kid gone, but I'll kill it in front of you if you don't fucking let me go." Harper only laughed. "You're going to jail for this. See if you don't. And once you're there, I'm going to take that baby from you even if I have to cut it from you myself. Let me go right now."

Harper looked at Grady. "What you said to her, is that really what you want? To raise my child as your own?" He said it was. "You don't know me. Nothing about me. For all you know, what she's saying could be true."

"Is it?" She shook her head at him. "I didn't think so. I want to care for you. Help you raise your son the best way we can. And someday, if you'll allow it, I'll marry you and give you both my name."

"What if you married me today?" He said he could arrange that. "You'd do that. Just like that, marry me."

"Yes. Today if we can—"

"You're not going to do any such thing. Harper, I swear to you, this is not going to end well for you. I just want you to pay what you owe me and then give the baby up. No one will ever know what sort of mistake you made in this."

"What sort of mistake do you think I made, Winnie? Trusting you? I didn't. And the fact that you had me taken from my own home by knocking me out wasn't bad enough. You then had me drugged and thrown in with a bunch of people I didn't know, to be impregnated by your husband's sperm. What about Scott and his wife? You had them killed too, didn't you, when they wouldn't tell you where I'd gone after you decided that you no longer wanted this child? You actually hired a guy to go hunting, and he killed them for you. Oh, I have no proof that you did it, but I know it was you." Harper wiped furiously at the tears that fell. "I think that goes a long way in saying just how much of a bitch you really are. What were you thinking? I told you no, that I didn't want to carry your child for you."

"I wanted this, and you were going to help me like I said from the start. You are such a cunt, Harper. I knew that all along, but the fact that you'd not help me out when I told you I needed you just goes to show what a selfish bitch you are. And so what? I've had a change of heart now, and you're still not doing as you're told. All you had to do was get rid of it. And when that didn't happen, I had to go to extreme lengths to get you to abort. Do you have any idea how much money I'm out because of what you've done to me? And even if I knew what you're talking about with those people, as you said, you have no proof." Harper looked at Grady. "Let me go and we'll settle this right now, Harper. I'm sick of messing with you."

The word abort hung in the air around her. Her sister had admitted to trying to make her miscarry her child. Harper felt the baby move, kicking under her hand, and she knew as surely as she was standing here that her sister was insane. Selfish and insane. The dragon, in a soft kind voice, told her that she and her son were safe now. But she wanted answers.

"Did you try to have me hurt? Did you actually try and have me lose this baby?" Her sister said nothing. Harper jerked her arm up tighter and was glad when she screamed. "I asked you a fucking question. Did you try and have me lose this baby?"

61

"Yes. But nothing worked. You'd think that you had someone watching over you the way you were able to thwart my efforts. My God, Harper, what does it take to have you do what I want?" Harper let her go and backed from her. "Now, we're going to settle this like adults. I have the paperwork in my car, and if you'll just write me a check after signing off on the contract, we'll part ways. I do hope you don't think to hold this against me. I certainly won't against you for how you've treated me. I did nothing that anyone in my position wouldn't have done. You're the one that has made this go all wrong. I keep telling you, Harper, do as I say and things will go better for everyone."

Harper looked at Grady and knew that nothing she did from here on out was as important as keeping her child safe.

"Marry me." She wasn't sure what spilled from her mouth, but the moment that it did, she could see the value in it. "Today if you can. I want this baby to have all the things he can that will keep him safe. And while I'm not completely sure why, I think marrying you can give that to him."

"All right." Grady looked at his mom, who was now standing with Kenton. "Can you help me out with this? I mean, it doesn't have to be huge, but later, if we want, you can fix that too. But we need a marriage license, as well as a reception afterwards please."

"Yes. I'll make some calls." His mom was pulling out her phone as she moved away from them. When she turned back, Harper just knew that she was going to say this was a bad idea. "Honey, please see to this trash. There is a nasty stench in here that is positively horrid."

She wasn't sure what was going on, but when Kenton helped Winnie up, Harper knew that Aisha was talking about her stinking the place up. Before she could move to the door to leave, her heart broken, Winnie was screaming again, this time at Kenton.

He was helping *her* out the door. Well, helping might have been the wrong word, but when he asked her to unlock it for him, Harper did so without thinking. Before she knew it, Winnie was out on the street on her ass, and Harper was being hugged by Grady.

"We'll make some arrangements today, and Mom can get us whatever we need to get married this afternoon. I know that you're going to need something to wear, a dress or something, so I'll have her take you to the local stores to get it." Harper nodded, enjoying the arms around her a little too much. "I just realized that I don't know what Kenton told you about your visit. Are the two of you all right? Do you need to rest or anything?"

It took her several moments to understand what Grady was saying. "Oh, the baby. He's fine. He said he was going to be a big boy, which surprised me since neither Winnie nor Jake are. And that I'm doing well. I have to rest more, but I'm healthy. Are you really going to marry me? Today?"

"Yes. I want you to understand that once the baby is born, he'll have my name. Are you all right with that?" She said that she was. "Good. I know nothing about babies, so you'll have to help me a little."

"I probably know less than you do. I don't have a lot of experience with babies or children. But I think, with your mom in our corner, we can't screw up too badly." He grinned at her. "You're very charming, did you know that?"

"You said I was a prick before. I think I like you calling me charming much better." Harper felt the baby move and rubbed her hand over him. When Grady asked if he could touch him as well, she took his hand under hers and put it over what she thought was a small foot. "I can feel him there. He's very active, isn't he?"

"He moves a lot when I'm stressed out. Not as much as before, but he gets around. Now that I know he's going to be big, I think he's running out of room." She felt the baby push against the hands over him. "I watch him move when I'm resting. He flips and flops around like a kid on a trampoline. I can't wait to see him. I mean, I know that he was unplanned, but I already love him with all my heart."

"Well, of course you do. This is the most amazing thing I've ever felt." She felt tears fill her eyes, blinding her for a moment with emotion. Grady wiped them away with his free hand and smiled at her. "You're so beautiful. Full of life, your body pink with health. I think I could easily love you for all time. I'm pretty sure I already do, as a matter of fact."

"Oh Grady, I do hope you don't regret this." He said he'd not, ever. "I hope not. You're the nicest person I've ever encountered. And I see a lot of people. But to do this for us, for my child, you have no idea how wonderful you've made me feel."

"We'll take care of you from now on, Harper. My family will be here for whatever you need." Harper laid her head on his shoulder, her body just overwhelmed with the kindness of a complete stranger. "We'll be fine, love. You'll see. And your sister will regret threatening me too. I'm not without my own resources."

She hoped so. Harper really did hope someone would help her out. Even if it was just for a little while.

CHAPTER 4

He looked at the notes that he'd been writing and realized that he had no idea what to do now. When he'd found her a few weeks ago he thought to kill her on site, take what he wanted, and leave her carcass for the rats to eat. But he wanted to play with her and the McCades. Just enough, he thought, to bring them out in force so that he could end them. But now she was gone and he didn't know who had helped her.

It was as if she'd had some magical being come to her hiding place and take her away right under his nose. Leaning back in his chair, he thought about what he was going to tell his buyer when he called. And he would, just as he had every night for the last two months.

Ollie Morrison was a man who got things done. Not with fanfare...there were no witnesses to his work. No one was looking for him, and he was positive that there wasn't another soul out there that had as much information about anything as he did. Ollie prided himself on knowing when, where, and how things were going to happen. It was why this thing with the woman was bothering him so much, not that anyone would be able to tell. But she had gotten away from him, and he'd lost a good bit of ground in getting the McCade jewelry. Not to mention, it was putting him behind. He had a plan and now it wasn't flowing the way he'd set up.

His temperament was calm, perfect really for his line of work. After numerous years of practicing how to look bored, to not show anger or happiness, Ollie knew that he had what would be considered the flawless poker face. And he liked it that way. When he sat at a table with buffoons, people who no more deserved to be near him than they did to be breathing his air, they would — out of respect for how good he was at everything — turn to him for solutions. And that was just the way he liked it.

But he'd lost the woman.

The notes that he'd taken seemed to tell him he'd missed something. She'd been in there not an hour before, nursing a wound that hadn't been in his plans either. Dead was fine, wounded was not. It left DNA behind, a way to track where she'd been.

The man, a boy really, had entered the room just before Ollie had been on his way to kill her and take what he wanted. Ollie had heard the woman tell the kid to get out when he was tossed out of the hotel room as if he were nothing more than an old newspaper. And then he just simply disappeared. Incinerated.

That too was something that he'd been pondering. What had killed him? When Ollie came upon his body as soon as it exited the room, he saw him. Only for a second, but it had been enough that he knew whatever power had killed him hadn't been human. His head had caved into his skull, and his chest, what was left of it, looked as if someone or something had reached into inside and pulled his heart free. It lay on his chest, just a mass of blood and a stringy mess, before it too had vanished in a puff of flame.

He'd backed away then. Gone back to his car to wait out

whatever had helped her. Nothing came out of the room after the door had been closed, and until he got the call from his business partner in his legitimate dealings telling him that he was needed, nothing had gone in either. Upon his return not two hours later, the room was devoid of even a fingernail. The towels too, anything holding any DNA, were missing. What sort of being could do that, he pondered?

His phone ringing startled him out of his thoughts. It was his buyer; Dave Hardy was right on time with his nightly call. Ollie didn't answer though. He had more important things to do at the moment than listen to the man whine.

Like where was the fucking girl? What had happened at the hotel? And where the fuck was the jewelry?

Pulling his phone closer to him, he thought of Bobby Ware. Fredrick, as he went by just before his death, had said that he was gathering the pieces for himself. He'd been good too; he'd not only had tabs on where one of the pieces of jewelry were, but he also had a lot of information that Ollie didn't. It took him nearly four hours to go through the dead man's house, and an hour more to put it all in the back of his car to bring here. Now it, along with the things that he'd gathered, were spread out around the room so that he could look them over.

"Where have you gone?" He knew that the McCades were more than likely aware of her. He wondered which of the four remaining men would take her into his home. He wouldn't have…not until he rid her of the bastard that she carried. But then he was funny like that, he thought with a laugh…he wasn't going to take anyone's sloppy seconds. "Not even a virgin, either."

Keeping tabs on the McCades had been a task that still gave him headaches. They came and went at all hours of the day and night. None of them seemed to have a job that would take them to a certain place at a specific time. He knew they were wealthy; not as much as he was, he thought, but they had disposable income. One of the women had inherited money from a couple of estates. But he never got a handle on who it might have been from, nor how much it was. He knew it wasn't in his ballpark, so he never cared that much to look.

He called the man he had watching over the family, and was pleased when he answered on the first ring. Ollie asked him how things were going on that end of his plans.

"The computer store is being worked on, as well as two other buildings across town. They're working all over the place, so it's hard for me to keep up with them." Ollie asked him if he wanted him to find a replacement. "No, no, I got it. Just letting you know. You don't have to go doing anything to replace me."

He'd kill him, and he was sure the man knew it. "I'm happy to hear that. What have you found out about the women of the family? Are they still making it difficult for you to get them separated from the men?"

"You'd think they'd want to go shopping or something like that. But they pretty much hang together. Even if they're with the elder McCade, there is someone forever trailing or with them as a driver. I'm thinking they know you're about." Ollie was sure they did not. He'd paid a great deal of money for keeping his part in finding the jewels a secret. "I have seen another woman there. Fat broad that's been hanging out with the computer guy."

Ollie sat up in his chair, and with a glance at the wall, knew which man it was. "Grady McCade. He is planning to open a computer store in seventeen days. What does the fat woman look like?"

"Pretty, but huge. I'm thinking that she's working on

losing some of it though. Every time I see her, she's walking to one of the buildings or another. She keeps this up and she'll shed it in no time. I had an aunt once that was well — "

"I'm sure that your aunt's astonishing weight loss is very intriguing. But this woman, is she pregnant or just simply fat? And is she beautiful, with long dark hair?"

"Could be. I never thought of her being heavy with child, but now that you mention it, they have been taking a little more care with how she gets to walking. Holding her hand when she crosses the street. Setting another chair in front of her when she plops down. Yes, sir, you could be right. She's not fat, but big with child." Ollie closed his eyes and thought of all the things he'd have to do now that she was with the McCades. "I can get you a picture if you want. I got a nice new cell phone to use when I talk to you."

"You're using a cell phone?" He said that was the only way that he could keep tabs on them and talk to him when he called. "You've been using one all along? A cell to call and send me.... Christ, did you send other pictures to my email address from it?"

"Of course. I don't have the money for a computer. You won't pay me until this is done, you said. And I'm okay with that, really I am, but you call at all hours of the night and day, and if I didn't have it, you'd never reach me. And I have to tell you, after I've seen how you deal with people that make you upset, I thought this was the best way."

Ollie disconnected the call. He was going to kill the man, then destroy his phone. It was too late to get the information from it; once it was out in the air, so to speak, it was there for anyone to see. But he wanted the man dead for being so incredibly stupid. As most people were.

Ollie had the information that he needed now. Even

some that he didn't. The fool had been broadcasting their conversations out to anyone that wanted to look. This was the main reason that he hated having people working for him. They were beyond stupid most of the time.

Ollie knew that at times he was a little paranoid. Like the cell phone usage. He hated using them. He could see the usefulness of them…like the man said, he was calling him all the time, but he didn't like them. Anyone could track him with a few key strokes, and it would be all over. Fuck the stupid man and his convenience.

Making arrangements to go to Ohio, Ollie thought of everything that he'd learned so far. Most of it was pretty farfetched, but there was some truth to it as well. Not that he really cared what the legend was or who was going to benefit from it. Ollie was selling the pieces to a single buyer on the pretense of knowing everything there was to know about the family and the jewels that came with them.

Who believed in dragons and magic? Not him, that was for sure. He'd heard there were shifters out in the world, things that would go from animal to another animal in no time at all. But he didn't believe it. He also heard that there were people out there that thought they were vampires. Others still that had it in their heads they were faeries, queens, and magical beings that could cast spells and do all manner of crap to someone. Ollie's only god was money, and he wanted more than anyone else.

Money could buy you anything you wanted. A new face, fingerprints, and identification to go with it. So in a way, it was just like a shifter to him. It could also buy you out of bad situations, guns if that didn't work, as well as a place to hide, lay low, and wait things out. Money, to him, was the cure all to everything. It was all he cared about. But he never seemed to have enough, and that bothered him.

Ollie made his arrangements. Flying wasn't his favorite way to travel, but he thought it necessary now. The latest McCade woman was fat with a child; whoever's it was would give him what he wanted or he'd kill her in front of him. Not that he wouldn't anyway, but he would use it to his advantage. Ollie didn't care who died or how, so long as he was able to come out on top.

Packing a bag for the trip seemed unnecessary, but he knew that to enter an airport with no baggage would get him flagged. Ollie was even flying second class — coach, he thought it was called — again so as not to draw attention to himself. Driving himself to the airport and parking his car in long term rather than taking a taxi was just another precaution that he took. Ollie was very good at keeping a low profile. It was why he was so good at what he did. Get the impossible before someone else did.

The flight, while short, was annoying. A woman and her several hundred children were an endless prattle of noise and crying. Not that she really had that many children, he thought — it was only the one — but it had annoyed him to no end that she couldn't keep one small being quiet long enough for him to rest. Inconsiderate people made him lose his temper faster than anything.

It had been his plan to make her trip up, or at least make the child scream once they landed. But a man, a very large one, sat down beside him and never moved, not even when Ollie told him, repeatedly, that he was invading part of his seat. Instead of moving, as he wished him to do, the man encroached in his area more. He was going to pay for this when they landed, Ollie was going to make sure of it.

Almost as soon as the plane touched down the man stood

up. Ollie did as well, and wasn't the least bit surprised to see that the man was taller than him. Not that it mattered; Ollie might be short on stature, but he was big on violence. However, just as he was going to hit the man in his cock, hoping to bring him to his knees, he looked him in the eyes.

The power of the gaze, the look that made Ollie feel as if he was looking as deeply into his soul as anyone had, made him take a step back. And when the man advanced toward him, just a single step in the overcrowded aisle, Ollie whimpered. He could no more have stopped it from spilling from his lips than he could the involuntary lift of his hands to shield himself.

"Touch her and you will die." He looked at the woman behind him, the one with the child, when the man spoke in such low tones. "Not her either, but I was talking about the McCade woman."

He started to tell him that he'd do what he wanted with her, that she had something that belonged to him. But he paused and thought, several things at once, as a matter of fact.

"Who are you?" The man only smiled, his sharp fake teeth glistening in the overhead light. "You're a fool if you think you can scare me with such a display. I don't believe in what you're showing me any more than I think you can stop me from my current path."

"Don't I? Don't I scare you, Ollie Herman Morrison?" Ollie felt his balls tighten to his body, sweat beading on his forehead. No one knew his full name and lived. His mother had yelled it out when she wanted him to come to her, and he had hated her enough to spit on her grave when she finally died. "I can smell you now. Fear. Did you know that it is as sweet to me as the taste of a fresh virgin?"

"I'm not afraid of you." The man laughed as he reached

into the overhead compartment and pulled out a single case. "You'd do well to stay away from me. I have very powerful friends that will stake you if I should want them to. I don't believe it will kill you…you're not what you're projecting. But it will humiliate you, and that is just as good."

"You have no such friends. You have no one at all." He looked at him again, the same dead look in his eyes that more than terrified Ollie. "Touch them, any of them, and I will enjoy taking you apart, piece by tiny little piece. And you can threaten me all you like…you'll still be a dead man that no one will ever find parts of."

Then he was gone. Ollie looked around and realized that he was the only one on the aircraft…even the staff had left him there. And the woman with the brat had gotten away as well. Ollie gathered his own case and was disembarking when he saw the small piece of paper in his jacket pocket. Pulling it out, he fell back against the wall when he saw what was there.

A picture of his office with all his notes hanging from pinup boards. Even the ones that he'd gotten from Fredrick. But it was what was written on the back that had him looking around. It was a list of the people that he'd killed over the last month and a half. The one on top, Bobby Ware, wasn't even the last one. Ollie was being followed.

~~~

Grady watched his friend coming down the long corridor. He'd called a month ago, begging him to come and help out with his new venture. Of course, Kurt had turned him down every time he asked, but just yesterday he'd called and said he was coming, and asked if he could be picked up at the airport.

"You have a nice flight?" He told him that he'd not, as a matter of fact. "It's because you're too large for the seats. I told you to stop being a cheap bastard and go to first class and you'd do well there. It's not...." He realized that Kurt wasn't paying any attention to him but staring at Harper who he'd made sit down to rest once they got here. "That is my future wife, Harper Bailey. We're waiting on tests and licenses right now. She and I are getting married—"

"She's being hunted; did you know that?" He told Kurt that he knew. "The man that I saw, he comes for her. He rode with me on the flight. He means to take her and the jewels from the rest of the women, and sell them off to the highest bidder."

"You know where he is now?" Kurt pointed to a shorter man wearing an impeccable suit. "He looks harmless enough. How do you know that he's looking for Harper?"

"I know." It was all the answer he was going to get, and really the only one he needed. If Kurt thought this man was going to be a danger to them, then he would be. "He is going to try and herd—his words, not mine—the young miss over there out of your reach and kill her. He doesn't have any idea what she has in the way of some jewelry, but he wants it. Perhaps you can help me understand why someone would kill a woman and her child over a bauble."

"It's not a bauble, but a relic of magic." He looked at Harper when she stood up. "Let's go to my house and I'll explain. Harper needs to rest."

Harper stood up when they reached her. He could feel her exhaustion, and even if he couldn't he would have seen it on every line of her face. She'd told him this morning that she wasn't sleeping well, and they were getting a new mattress for her as soon as they dropped Kurt off at his house.

"Grady said you were a vampire. I was curious why you can be outdoors." Grady smiled when her face turned pink. "I'm sorry. Since I've become this cow, I don't seem to be able to filter what I say anymore. You don't have to answer the question. I was rude, and I'm sorry."

"It's all right, my lady. I think you're refreshing. But to the reason why I can be out so early in the day is because I'm not wholly a vampire. I have a little of this and that in me." She asked him what he meant, and Grady wasn't sure he was going to answer her. He did, but waited until they were in the car. "My mother was a half breed…part vampire and the other part faerie. My father, a man of considerable age and power, was a warlock. He passed to me a variety of things, one of which is the power to withstand a great deal of sunlight, as well as the ability to have a fine meal with a beautiful woman should I want."

"You're full of malarkey, as my grandma would say." Kurt laughed and when he did, Grady joined him. Kurt looked at him, just shaking his head as Harper continued. "So you're a mutt, so to speak. I am as well. Part German, Irish, and Dutch, and then there is a small mixture of Native American and a touch of Welsh. I'm not sure that any of them gave me any special powers, but here I am."

"There you are. And your child, do you know what he is? I can tell you should you like to know." She looked at Grady and then back at Kurt. "Have I fallen into more trouble than the man on the plane?"

"Yes. My sister is a peach, and not the warm and fuzzy sort. More like the pit and any rotten places you might find on it. My brother-in-law as well." Grady drove them to the shopping center, as Kurt said he needed a few things as well, while Harper explained. "So as you can tell, she is not on my list of favorite people right now."

"No, I would imagine not. But should you need me to go and find them, sort of put them on the straight and narrow,

I would gladly do so." Harper told him she'd think about it. "So this jewelry that is causing the uproar...I have read the mind of the man who would pursue you, and he has it that he wishes to sell it. To a buyer that has his sights set on keeping it until the next generation of McCades were born. This isn't the legend of the demi parvure, is it?"

"It is. I'm surprised you know anything about that." Kurt told him that he had read about it in passing. "Passing or not, if you have any information at all on this, it's more than we have been able to find out."

They shopped for a mattress for nearly two hours. It wasn't that hard; on the contrary, it was a blast. Kurt had Harper laughing by the time they'd made their first foray into testing the mattresses out, and kept them both entertained while they not only purchased one, but also a crib and other baby furniture.

"I was wondering if you'd do me a favor, my lady." Kurt looked at him, then back at Harper. "This man, he will come for you, and while I know that you are stronger than he thinks, I should like to taste a little of your blood...nothing to harm the child, but enough so that I can find you, or talk to you should you need it. Grady and I have exchanged blood before, on numerous occasions."

"He saved my life, and I returned the favor when he was nearly too weak to go on." Harper didn't say anything as they stood in the nursery department, but continued to turn her back to them. "Harper, is everything all right?"

"I'll let you do this, taste my blood, if you do me a favor." Kurt, of course, told her anything. "Don't say that too fast, please. I want to make sure that if there is a reason for you to have to find me, you make sure that my son is all right first. I know that I never wanted him, not at all, but now that he's here, within me, I find that I'm kinda glad for it."

She turned to them then, and Grady could see the fear and determination in her eyes. Kurt took her hand to his mouth and kissed the back of it before turning it over to see her palm. He touched the small pulse there at her wrist, running his fingers over it several times as he stared at her.

"I can see into your life. Not all your future, but enough to know that you and your child are well cared for and loved. Nothing too harmful will come to either of you." Before Grady could ask him what that meant, Kurt continued. "You will be injured, I'm afraid. You and your son, but neither of you will be killed by it nor maimed badly."

"Will the outlook change if I let you take my blood?" Kurt grinned and told her she was much too smart for her own good. "Yet you didn't answer me. You taking my blood…will it save my son from harm?"

"Yes, my lady, it will save you both." Harper told him to do it. "I should warn you that all things come with a price. I will not only be able to find you should you want, but feel you as well. Every emotion that you have, as well as when you are dying. Not that I foresee that happening, but I wanted you to know that."

"You mean when I'm having a shitty day or just hormonal?" Kurt had given him the same warning when they'd exchanged blood. "I want you to do this, but I'd like something in exchange. A boon, I think it's called. I want you to make sure that no matter what, you never put yourself in harm's way to save me. Not to the point where you might not make it out alive."

Kurt looked at him, then at Harper. "I'm sorry, my dear, but I cannot do that. You are, as of the moment that I met you, a being that I would die for. For you and the child. I will not allow harm to come to either of you, for the simple reason that you are the mate to my dearest friend."

"Don't be hurt, please?" Kurt said he would try his very best. "You can take my blood, but know this; I won't allow you to come to harm either if I can help it."

Kurt licked her wrist and then bit gently into her flesh. She wasn't in pain...Grady knew that Kurt would never harm her, and when he licked the wound closed, he looked at him and smiled. There was something about it that made him feel like Kurt had a secret. And when he nodded at him, Grady said they'd talk later, that they had a baby to buy for.

CHAPTER 5

Dalton made sure the new guest in the little bed and breakfast was where he was supposed to be before going home for the day. Ollie Morrison was an odd duck, as his grandda would have said, but no less dangerous for how he looked. As he made his way back to his offices after setting up a member of the local pack in the B&B to help out, he reached out for Kenton and told him what was going on.

Thank you. I know that you're being overworked right now, what with Howard gone, but I appreciate you for making sure this guy is away from Harper. I had to put her on bed rest this morning, and as you can imagine, she didn't take that well. Dalton laughed, telling him he would imagine she was very vocal about it. *Yes, and she threatened me. But as soon as Grady talked to her, it was like she'd never been pissy. Hormones are a very scary thing.*

He'd figured that out last night when he'd been talking to Harper about her sister. She sobbed the entire conversation and kept telling him she was fine. He had no idea why, but he felt like he should stand himself in the corner for making her cry like she had.

As soon as he pulled into his driveway, Dalton sat there for several minutes just staring up at his home. He tried to think what it was he was supposed to be doing tonight. He knew that he had some sort of engagement or appointment, but for the life of him, all he could think about was his nice soft bed. When his phone rang he growled low and pulled it out to see who it might be. Unknown popped up, but he answered anyway.

"McCade." There was someone talking in the background, a voice he didn't know and noises that he thought were from a restaurant. Dalton waited before speaking again, trying to get an idea on who it might be. And when the woman spoke, he thought of nails on a chalkboard.

"I'm looking for Kenton McCade." Dalton said nothing to the woman. His number was listed, Kenton's wasn't. "I want to talk to Kenton McCade. Can you tell me how to reach him?"

"How do you know that's not who you're talking to now?" She asked him if he was Kenton. "What is it you want? You called me, why?"

"My sister. She's got it in her head that she can keep that baby from me. I wanted her to abort it when she was still early in this mess, but she had to play hardball with me. I'm telling you right now, Harper is nuts if she thinks I won't win in this. So, if this is Kenton, I can make it worth your while to give it to me when she gives birth. How much would it cost to have you slip it to me while she's drugged up?" Dalton was shocked and pissed when she laughed. "Come on now, surely you have a price that'll make you help me? Or to look the other way. I need that baby gone, and I'd very much like for you to help with that."

"You want me to give you a child that doesn't belong to you, and you'll pay me for it?" She asked him again what his price would be. He started to tell her there wasn't one when he realized that he could take care of this right now. "I don't know how much it would be. A lot. I have student loans to take care of."

He got out of his car and made his way to the house. Dalton was both startled and glad to see Jorden there, and he told him what was going on. Jorden asked to listen in as he and this woman spoke.

"My husband and I need some reassurances first. One, that you won't come back for more money. We have solid reputations to make sure aren't damaged with this. And secondly — and this should have been first — is that you never tell anyone what we've done. You would be in as much trouble as we are should you speak about this to anyone anyway, but you're to keep your trap shut on this." He asked her if she'd tell anyone. "Good heavens, no. I want that thing gone and out of my life. I have no idea why Harper wouldn't do this for us in the first place, but now that it's done, she's acting like it was all her idea, and thinks she's going to raise it with that man from the computer store. Christ, a computer store manager trying to raise a child? What sort of salary do you suppose he gets?"

"I think he owns the building and store, as a matter of fact." She just laughed and said that was doubtful. It occurred to him that the other day when Winnie had been at Grady's store that she hadn't caught their last name. Otherwise, he was sure that she'd have connected Kenton to Grady, and wouldn't have tried to contact him to get him to do something so underhanded as to kidnap her sister's child. "I'm going to see Harper in the morning, and I'll let you know after that. It will depend on how she treats me."

"She's a bitch, in the event you might have missed that. And while you're checking her out, if she happened to deliver a baby that wasn't breathing, I'd not be overly distraught about that either."

Dalton looked at Jorden when the line was disconnected. "Do you suppose she has any idea that she's not only just talked to a cop, but has prearranged a murder as well as a kidnapping?" Dalton told Jorden he wouldn't think so. "Yeah, me either. Christ, this woman is seriously stupid if she thinks any of us would do something so horrific to our sister-in-law."

"I don't think she knows." Jorden asked him what he meant and he explained. "She thinks she got a doctor that might be caring for Harper. There aren't any more in this area, as you know, so she's assuming, and rightly so, that Kenton is her physician. Winnie thinks Kenton is going to help her, and she has no idea that we're all related."

"The wedding is tonight." Jorden looked at his cell phone. "In an hour. I came by to pick you up while Jasmine and Emma get Harper ready."

"Christ, that was it." Dalton told Jorden that he'd remembered that there was something, just not what it was. "I've been so overworked lately. I cannot wait for Howard to get back from vacation so I can be just a regular cop again. This being in charge shit is for the birds."

"But you do it so well, little brother." Dalton flipped him off. "Also, you should know that if this thing ever comes to a head, which I have no doubt it will, neither Winnie nor her husband are going to have shit. Mom has made a few calls."

"Christ, then they're as good as done." He was still standing there, trying to think what he'd been about to do, when Jorden reminded him he was going to the wedding. "I need a break, Jorden, and a long nap."

As he was getting dressed for the wedding, which was being held at his mom's house, he told Kenton what had transpired. Kenton was obviously pissed off, but also told him not to tell either Grady or Harper until after the wedding.

I think this sister is going to be as much trouble, if not more than, the dragon killers. Dalton agreed with him. *Also, did you know that Kurt is in town? I thought he was here for the wedding, but he came to talk to Grady about another matter. The guy has had some rough times lately. I guess he's wanting to settle down and be a regular person. Try and come to terms with all that's happened to him lately.*

I believe you might be right. I read about his brother last night on the computer. For as nice a guy as Kurt is, I can't believe what an ass his brother is. Kenton told him that he'd heard not an hour ago that David was dead. *Well, I can't say that I'm surprised by it. But, no, I hadn't heard. What was it? Did he get killed in prison?*

No, though I'm betting he had wished he had been. The council brought their judgment against him. And you know as well as I that they're swift with their punishment. I guess he was taken from his cell to the courthouse, and never made it. Dalton said that was the way he'd want to go, quick and done. *I doubt it was quick, but it's done. I guess Kurt felt it.*

I'll see what I can find out for him if he wants. That guy has had a really terrible year so far.

Kenton said he'd see him at Mom's just as Dalton and Jorden were getting into Jorden's truck. Dalton told him what was going on. As soon as they pulled into Mom's drive, he knew that something else had happened, and he had a feeling that it was the sister. The bitch hadn't waited until later.

Thankfully, it hadn't been that at all, just a slight mishap with the cake. Lewis had miscalculated the amount needed, and he and Emma had baked cupcakes to take up the slack. It was going to be one hell of a reception if those two were in charge of the food, Dalton thought.

~~~

Harper looked down at the white dress she had on without

really seeing it. She was trying to think past the pain in her heart over what her sister had done to her. To think that they had the same blood, the same parents even, and were so very different. Harper looked up when someone said her name. It was Emma

"You okay?" Harper said she wasn't sure. "Yeah, I can understand that. She does know how to make someone simply want to run her through, don't you think? If I had a sister like her.... Hey, I had a brother like her. He wasn't as smart as your sister appears to be, but just as evil. Can I do anything for you?"

"No. I'm not sure this is such a good idea now. I mean, she said she was going to get all of us in trouble." Emma sat on the chair across from her, her belly just beginning to show a little, and Harper thought her adorable. "Grady should have someone that's normal."

"Normal? I'm not even sure that word fits any of us. Not anymore. Did you know that when I first came here, I thought I was insane? Well, I was, I guess. Sick too, and hurting. The building that I was in blew up because someone thought that my brother, Bart, and I had killed our mother. Who, I might mention, was still very much alive."

"Mmm, yeah." They both laughed. "Grady is such a nice man. He's spent so much money on this baby, and it's not even his. I hate that he might have wasted his money."

"I don't think he would feel that way if you asked him." Harper had, and he said it had been fun. "I don't doubt that he thought so, and would have spent more if you wanted something else. Besides, I have it on good authority that he's been reading up on how to handle a baby. He said that he's not had a lot of experience, and has been also bugging his mom about things. That doesn't sound like a man who thinks he wasted his money on baby items and diapers."

"I asked him to marry me." Emma said she knew that as well. "What do you think of that? A desperate woman asking your brother-in-law to marry her so that her sister can't take the baby she had implanted without consent?"

"I think you've been dealt a shitty hand, and now that you're here with us, things will turn around. Not all at once, mind you, but it will get better."

Harper asked her how she knew that. Instead of answering, Emma put her hand on her belly. The baby kicked then…he'd been doing that off and on since she sat down. When Emma smiled at her, Harper put her hand over Emma's and moved it to the left, enough to feel him flip again.

"Do you know what I think right now?" Harper shook her head. "I think that this little man is going to be so loved, so happy, that he won't care at all that his aunt is a fucking bitch, and I don't mean me or Jasmine. He'll be smart, like his daddy, Grady, and handsome like his uncles. He might know about his other aunt, the bitch this time, but he won't care. Not one bit, so long as his mommy is happy and daddy loves him. Do you love him, Harper?"

"Yes I do. I didn't want to, but from the moment that he moved, that first little blip, I fell right over in love with him." Emma said that was the way it should have been. "What about Winnie? She's not going to give up, you know. And to be honest, Emma, I'm so tired of her shit that I just want to find a gun and shoot at her. Not hit her…that would be wrong, but at her enough so she'll know that I mean business."

"Oh, I hope she doesn't give up, because the moment she comes here there will be a reckoning like she's never seen. Not only will someone shoot at her, but I'm pretty sure that she'll go running with her tail between her legs so quickly that all we'll see is a trail of smoke. They'll both be sorry they ever tangled with this family." Emma leaned in and so did Harper. "Have you seen the dragons yet? Grady's, I mean?"

"No." Her voice, like Emma's, was a whisper. "Are they real? I mean, I know that you believe in them, but have you seen them?"

"Oh my, yes. I'm married to the king of them. And so you know, Jasmine's baby is more dragon than the rest of them. I don't know about you, but I'm as excited as hell that we're going to have dragons around. Not just our mates, but children too. Won't that be just wonderful?"

They were both laughing when Aisha came in to tell them that it was time. Harper was finally allowed to see herself; the mirror had been covered when they helped her dress. So when she stood and the drape was taken off, Harper could only stare at the reflection that was in front of her. It was hard to realize that it was her. Rubbing her hand over her belly again, she assured the little man there that things were going to be just fine.

And they will be, my lady. There are things in the works now that will bring another piece to the family soon. I know not what it is yet, but it has been found and the wearer is...well, I meant to say she is as stubborn as you, but I don't think that's possible.

"She's not putting it on either, is she? How do you know that she's the one then? I mean, it could be in a box that she just happens to be near." She'd only been kidding, but apparently dragon took what she said to heart. "This woman, she'll be fine, right?"

Yes, she will be once she is on her way. Harper told him to keep her safe as well. *I will, my lady. I will. And when she gets here, when she has found her mate, I should like for you and the other women to help her. I'm not sure what it is she needs help with, but I*

feel sorrow from her, a great deal of it. And as she will not wear her
piece, I cannot tell what it is or what has her so sad.

"We'll be here for her." Harper knew that they all would,
just as they'd been for her. And her sister, Winnie, and her
asshole husband could go straight to hell.

The wedding went off without a single mishap. Grady
had looked so handsome standing up there with his brothers
that she paused as she made her way out of the front room.
Kurt had volunteered to give her away...she had no one else,
and when he said her name softly she had looked up at him.

"They're a family. I mean, I know that, but they're really a
good family." Kurt said that they were hers now. "Will you be
mine as well, Kurt? I know that we've only just met, but will
you be my...I guess my brother?"

"I am older than that by a considerable amount, Harper,
but I would be honored to call you my sister." He kissed her
hand and she smiled at him. "Now, let's get you wed and a
McCade so that your baby has a strong name too."

At the reception, Harper felt the first cramp in her back
and let out a long breath when it seemed to make her woozy.
Grady was there beside her as they greeted his friends as they
congratulated them. When a second cramp took her breath
away, she found herself being lifted up and carried away at a
dizzying speed. She looked up at Grady when he put her on
a bed.

"I hurt." He took her hand in his and kissed it, softly
like he had when they were wed. "Grady, we have guests
downstairs. This isn't a good time for me to be—"

The pain was horrific. She screamed with it. And when
she looked at Grady again, she noticed that he was as white as
the dress she had on. Something was wrong, something with
the baby.

"Harper, look at me." She tried to scream again, but the pain was in waves now. "Harper McCade, look at me."

The voice, the authority in it, had her turning to Kenton. She told him she hurt and he said that it was natural in child birth.

"No, you said I had two weeks. You said I wouldn't go for two weeks. I'm holding you to that, Kenton…you said I'd have plenty of time." He laughed and she grabbed a handful of his hair. "I don't think you want to laugh right now."

He peeled her fingers off his hair and told her to be calm. She was pretty sure that when she got up she was going to murder him, and she told him that…loudly, she was pretty sure.

"Harper, you need to calm down, you're hurting the baby." She looked at Grady, at his calm face. "Just breathe in and out for me, and that'll help Kenton with his exam."

"Yes, he'll tell me that it's only false labor, right?" Grady told her to breathe…he even did it with her. "I feel better now. Thank you for taking me away. I feel just horrible that I had to embarrass you, today of all days."

"You'd never embarrass me. Kenton did once. He thought it would be funny to dress up as Mom and come to my parent-teacher meeting. It didn't go over that well." Another pain took her, but with Grady there telling her to breathe and to talk to, she got through it better this time. "Mom was fit to be tied. I don't know whether she beat him or not, but she was really pissed for a year at him."

"Mom was pissed at you too, if I remember." Grady told Kenton to shut up. "I'll tell you later, Harper, it's funny. Right now, let's have a baby, shall we?"

"What happened to the two weeks?" He laughed again and she decided that she hated him a great deal. Then another pain took her and she had to work hard at keeping herself from screaming again. She had a feeling that she was scaring Grady.

The pain was overwhelming at times, and not so bad others. Kenton asked her if she wanted something for pain, and she thought maybe she'd asked him about how it would affect the baby. If he told her she had no idea, but a few minutes later she wasn't hurting and she closed her eyes. Grady said her name twice and she had to pry her eyes open to look at him.

"You're doing fine, Harper. Kenton said it won't be long now." She nodded, or thought she did, then ice was shoved in her mouth. It was like cheesecake with cherries on it and the best beer she'd ever drank at the same time.

"Is he all right?" Grady told her they were both doing fine, and again that it wouldn't be long now. "We didn't talk about names. I never thought of one either, to be honest, and I've had a lot longer to think about it."

"What about your parents? Your father's name?" She said that he'd not hung around much after she was born. "All right. Is there someone you admire? Perhaps a very good friend?"

"You." The pain was dull but she could feel it. It was different too, like she needed to bear down. Looking at Kenton when he told her it was time, she asked him what she had to do.

"Just push him out. Like you have to take a hard poop." She'd heard that before, or had read about it, and nodded once. "All right, Harper, when you're ready I want you to bear down hard. It's time I get to meet my nephew."

Pushing was hard work. She was hot and sweaty most of the time, and when he told her not long now, she tried to tell him to fuck off. But Kenton was there for her, just as Grady was, and she did just what they told her. And when Kenton said push once again, Harper felt the baby leave her body.

His screams made her laugh. Her son, her little man, had been born. As she laid there, her body suddenly weak with exhaustion, she held onto Grady's hand. She wanted to see him, and sleep too, but Grady said that he just wanted to be by her for a moment or two longer. Then the baby was there.

Someone had pulled her dress down so that the moment the baby touched her skin, Harper knew a happiness that she'd never known before. Her baby boy was born, and he was all right. Grady kissed her when she laughed, and the two of them sobbed like small children when he cried out again. Then she had him count his fingers and toes. Harper cried once more when Grady told her they were all accounted for.

"What's your middle name?" Grady told her it was Shawn. "Then if you don't mind, I'd like to name him Shawn Grady McCade. That's a good strong name, one he can be proud of for the rest of his life."

Grady kissed her then, warmly and full of love. Shawn cried out and Kenton told her to try and nurse him. Getting him to her breast proved to be much harder than she thought it would be, but with Grady helping her, Shawn finally latched on and began nursing. It was the oddest feeling in the world to have someone suckle at her breast.

Harper must have drifted in and out. She was moved once, her body lifted up, and then she was laid back on soft sheets. A few ice chips were given to her, and she answered some questions before she fell asleep again. The baby, her Shawn, was safe, she knew this, and let the exhaustion of the last few months take her under.

When she woke, there was someone in the room with her. Always Grady, she noticed, but the others were taking turns sitting with them. Once it was Aisha, and she held Shawn in her arms. Another time it was Emma, and then the brothers. Every time she woke to see them there, they would reassure her that everything was all right and that Shawn was here with her. And once, the dragon spoke to her.

You have done well, my lady. Your son, he will be a strong McCade and keep his siblings safe. She asked him if she was going to have other children. *Yes. You and Grady will have several male children. All of them fine boys. You will also have a daughter, who will be a fine addition to the family line.*

Harper thanked him and closed her eyes again. Dragon said something about his strength, and that he was stronger because of the band on her arm, but she was just too tired to care. This time when she closed her eyes, she knew it was the last time for a while.

CHAPTER 6

Winnie held her body as stiff as she could while they were fussing with her hair and dress. She'd been at this for hours and was tired and hurting. She was also starving, but she'd never tell them that. To be hungry was a part of her life. And Winnie was determined to not let a little thing like food make her less than perfect.

"Winnie, I need you to look less pissed off. The furrows between your eyes look like mountain slopes." She wanted to tell him to fuck off, that she had a lot on her mind, but she only worked at smoothing out the frown that was her sister's fault. "That's better. Not perfect, but better."

The camera made noises. Not that it needed to, but whatever setting it was on made her think of drills in the dentist office. And she'd been there a lot over the first part of her career, making her as beautiful as she could be. Perfect. Winnie had had a lot of work done to her face and body over the years, and it had paid off. She was flawless, her body hard with muscles that working out for ten hours a day when she wasn't modeling had given her.

When the set was done, she was helped down off the platform she'd been put on and to her chair again. It was going to be a long day, with three photographers taking shots for different magazine covers and dress designs that she would be the cover model for. The one coming up would be more draining than the first had been, she knew, but she was perfect and the cameras loved her.

Her cell phone ringing had her shooing away the hair stylist. It was Jake, and she wanted to find out if he'd been made an offer as yet where he worked. It was well past time they promoted him by giving him this partnership. Winnie was already planning a huge party to celebrate it. People who weren't invited would be so jealous, too. As soon as she answered she knew that it was bad news.

"They said that they're going to wait another week before making the decision. I don't know why they feel they must delay, but they said something more had come in and they wanted to investigate it thoroughly before picking the new partner. I'm certain that it's to do with Manson. The man has more skeletons in his closet than I do shirts in mine." She asked him if he'd told them anything about the new house they were thinking of buying. "No. I started to, but then Pine said that his wife was having a child any day now, and I wasn't sure a new house could top that. It would for you and me, but they were all over Pine like he'd invented pregnancy. Christ, I wish we'd never thought of talking to your sister about this. I think she's going to ruin us all with her lies. I don't suppose you heard anything from that doctor, did you?"

"No, not yet. But I think I've convinced that idiot to help us out. He's telling me that he wants a million dollars. He'll never collect, but he can want all he needs to until I get what I want. And I will have that brat." Winnie looked around and lowered her voice. "I've got someone to take the kid once he brings it to me. They're willing to take it off my hands for less than what Harper owes us, and then kill off the good doctor while making it look like an accident. Then once she pays us, we'll about break even." Jake asked her if she'd gotten any word on the money. "No, but I will soon. If she thinks she can just not pay us back for all we went through, then she's stupider than I thought. To think that we went to a lot of expense for her and this is how she repays us."

Winnie looked at her reflection in the mirror and tried to stretch her neck muscles out to keep them supple. Her face was her money maker, her body the gravy. Just three more years of this and she and Jake would be millionaires, with a nice house and cars, as well as servants.

Winnie realized that Jake was speaking and told him to repeat himself because she'd been busy with someone.

"I said that the house that we wanted has been sold. I just got the email." She asked him if he knew who had bought it and for how much. "It looks like about ten grand more than we had offered. Damn it, that house was perfect for us. I have to see about.... The second house we put an offer on is off the market too, it says here. Well, that's odd."

She waited for him to explain and waved the stylist to come back. Whatever he said now wasn't going to be a secret for much longer anyway. They were buying a house, so what. It was what couples who had it all did. As her hair was curled in a style no human could ever do on their own, she listened to Jake as he told her about the third house that they'd looked at.

"I just got an email from the realtor that we were using. She said that she can't help us find a house any longer. Something about a conflict of interest." Winnie told him to call her and find out. "I will. There are three more houses in that area within our price range. I'll set up a time with her to see them as well. Whatever her conflict is, she'll just have to deal with it on her own time. We need to find the perfect house."

"It'll have to be this week. Next week I'm flying to Paris for the spring fashion event." He said that he'd remembered. "Also, Jake, have you heard from anyone concerning that other matter? I've been tied up here all day."

"No. Nothing. He told you that it would be two more weeks, right? Before anything happened?" She said that was what he said when he called her back a few hours after she'd first called him. "Winnie, you were brilliant in finding the number and calling that guy. To think we could have had him where we wanted him all along. I just wish we didn't have to pay him to do this for us. You'd think he'd want things to be right for people like us. Harper won't go away, and that's just not right of her."

"Some people just don't understand what it's like to be us, Jake. And as I said, he won't have anything to worry about when it comes to his share in all this." When she told him she had to go, Winnie leaned back on the chair and closed her eyes. Makeup was being applied to her face, something dramatic no doubt, and she let them do their thing. While that was being done, Winnie thought of her sister and the mess she'd put them in.

Harper had always been jealous of her. And after their mom had been killed, she'd been too clingy for Winnie to stand. Putting her with people that could handle the ugly duckling, which Winnie had always thought of her sister as being, hadn't been nearly as hard as getting her taken to the clinic she'd set up for her. Harper was the most ungrateful person she'd ever met.

When the makeup artist and stylist were done with her, she made her way to the set. Her assistant was right behind her, just how Winnie liked it, when Karl, the photographer, stepped in front of her. Taking several steps back, she bumped into the woman behind her and nearly fell on her ass.

"Karl? What is it? You nearly mussed me. I thought we were meeting on the bridge." He shook his head, the grin on his face not telling her anything. "I'm on my way now if you'd like to go there with me."

"We're done." She asked him what he meant. "Telling you this will be the most fun I've had in a while, but I've no need for you on the set today, Winnie. You're finished."

She'd never cared for this particular photographer. He thought that his photos were the best in the world, and had told her on numerous occasions that she should only have him shoot her. Winnie had never understood how he figured that was going to work when the man wouldn't leave the state he'd been born in. Not to mention, he had a real phobia of sand. Who was afraid of sand? So, it was understandable that he was pissy with her whenever they had to work together.

"I don't understand. Am I coming back?" He moved then, his body angled in a way that she was sure he'd done it on purpose. Winnie saw her then...Dani West was standing in the spot she'd been going to, wearing the same dress and makeup. "What is she doing here? And why is she taking my shots?"

"As I said, you're finished. Dani is going to be taking all your appointments today. And I have a message that you're to call your agent as soon as possible. I do believe you've been outed." She asked him what he meant as Dani was posed for her shoot. She was doing it all wrong, and even from this distance, Winnie could see it. "Someone, very high on the ladder, has called in some favors, and I do believe that your career is over."

"Who would do something like that? And who did you hear this from?" He said that a little birdy told him. "Well, I don't believe you. I want you to hold my job open for me while I make a few calls."

He simply walked away from her. It was in her contract that no one was to do that unless she gave them permission. But right now she was too upset to blast him as she normally would have. Pulling out her phone again she called Taylor, her agent.

"I'm glad you've called me. I was just now sending you back your contracts. I've been told, and none too gently either, that you and I are finished." Winnie asked her why someone would do that. "I have no idea, Winnie, but whoever you pissed off is really out to get your ass. And I have it on good authority that your husband is going to be out as well. What the fuck did you do?"

"Nothing. I have...this has to be a mistake, Taylor. I'm perfect. Jake is perfect. It's why we married." She only snorted at her. "I'll get to the bottom of this. Just don't do anything rash. I'm sure that it's only a mistake. Like perhaps they got the wrong name or something. I'm the best thing to hit modeling in a long time, and I have no doubt that this is simply an error."

"If you say so. In the meantime, my phone is ringing off the hook with people telling me to cancel whatever they have going with you. And as I said, I heard that Jake is on the out list too. You guys had better start gathering your wagons, my dear. There is a huge assed shitstorm coming, and it's headed right for Mr. and Mrs. Perfect." There was a tone there, but one that Winnie chose, for now, to ignore. She had more important things to worry about. Like who was making her life difficult.

It took her nearly two hours to get home. The limo service that she'd come to the set in was no longer available to her. The outfit that she'd worn had been taken away as well. They were set props, she'd been told, and she'd have to make do. Whatever that meant…Winnie hadn't made do in a decade. Not since she'd gotten her breasts enhanced. Even her makeup bag and its contents were taken from her. Christ, this was a mess.

Jake called her as soon as she got into a cab. Winnie was sickened by the smell. She was nearly in tears when she asked the man to please stop and get something to freshen it up for her. All he did was turn the heat up…like it wasn't bad enough in there, the heat only made it worse.

"I just heard from the firm. I've been fired, Winnie. They said they had information on me that made me an unlikely candidate for not only partnership, but also to work there. Winnie, I've never lost my job before." She told him what had happened on the set. "What's going on? Who would do this to us?"

"I don't have any idea. It has to be a mistake. We have to figure this out, Jake. I can't not work. We have no money." For the first time since she'd left home, Winnie was afraid. Not just because she was out of work right now, but the thought of having no money scared her to death. "Did they say anything to you? Give you any idea who it might be that has targeted us?"

"No. All Allen said was they had information and that it wasn't good. I asked him what it might be and he told me to contact the attorney that had called him." She asked him if he'd called yet. "No, I was waiting on you to be here. Hurry home, Winnie. We have to get this fixed. Oh, and I'm not going to get my severance pay nor my final check. What sort of fucked up shit is that?"

She wanted to be anywhere but at her home right now. There were things that she had to understand, things to settle up. Winnie wanted to be on a shoot, wanted to be making arrangements for Paris next week, not worrying about why she and her husband were suddenly out of work. Whatever Jake had done to do this to her, he'd better have a way of fixing it. Winnie wanted her money and fame back.

~~~

Harper watched Grady with the baby. Shawn was laying on a changing table and Grady was standing over him changing his diaper, she thought, and talking to him. She had to smile when she heard him telling the little man to make sure he told his mom that he loved her every day.

Harper thought about the people that had come to her aid in the last few weeks. Not only had they helped her have a beautiful wedding, but they'd made sure that her and Shawn got the best of care, as well as pampered like she was a queen. And Grady had been right beside her every step of this new journey. He smiled at her when he turned and caught her staring at him.

"Shawn has been a really good boy today. He let my mom give him a sponge bath, and he didn't pee on her this time. Also, Kenton said that he's in wonderful shape and didn't need to see him officially for another month. However, he said that he'll be over later just to be his uncle." She took Shawn when he handed him to her. "I think he's hungry. I love watching him eat his hands, but I don't think he's going to be satisfied with that much longer."

As soon as she bared her breast for her son, he latched onto her nipple like he'd been starved. While he settled into his meal, she looked around for something to cover herself with. Grady asked her please not to do that.

"I can't feed him, not like you can, so I have to take what I can get. Mom said that I could give him a bottle when you're busy, but I really love watching you nurse him." Harper looked at the baby rather than Grady. The man was just too nice, she thought. "I have some things to tell you. A lot of it you're not going to like, but you have to know. My mother, she has some long reaching arms and she's done a few things."

"Am I going to be in trouble with her?" He laughed and told her not ever again. "She said that to me, last night when she came to see us. She said that I had some grandma points in reserve. I wasn't sure what she meant, so she explained. By making her a grandma with Shawn, she said that she's set aside some points for me. And that will keep me out of hot water so long as I have points. Sort of like a payment plan for fucking up, I guess."

"She told me the same thing. Only I don't have as many. I'm just the father and you'd given birth. Shawn peeing on her, she told me, added points to his reserve rather than taking them away, because he'd marked her. My mom is odd." Grady was taking on the role of being Shawn's father like he really was. "My mom called in a few favors, as I said, such as Jake's firm and asked them to look into a few things. I think he might be out of a job soon."

"Why would she do that? I mean, I don't care for the man, but your mom, she doesn't know him." Grady helped her change breasts when Shawn fussed. When he was eating again, she looked up at Grady. "I don't want your mom getting into trouble over this thing with my sister. Aisha has been wonderful to us, and I don't want her to feel obligated to help me out."

"My mom, I'm sure you'll figure out, never does things

unless she wants to. And I think this was something that needed to be done. Did you know that there was an outrage at the college that Jake went to? That he and a group of others were accused of cheating on their exams?" Harper said she'd not heard that. "I didn't think so because there was a large donation made to the college by their parents. It was basically shoved under the rug and wiped from the books."

"Then how did your mom find out? She didn't pay someone, did she?" Grady shook his head and said that Kurt knew. "He read his mind."

"Yes. It was quite a scandal, I guess. Jake and his buddies not only cheated on the exam, but it turns out that they had some pretty damaging parties that cost his parents a great deal of money. Kurt was also able to unearth a few mail frauds that Jake has been a part of since he's been at the firm he's at now. Jake was there—and this is only what my mom found out—and getting the partnership from because Winnie nagged them so much. They figured it was easier to just give it to him and shut her up. I'm doubting that would have done it. She, from my experience with her, never has enough." Harper asked him what else. "I'm assuming you're asking me about your sister?"

"Yes. I have a feeling that she's…. What was he was able to find on her? I'm sure that there is something. Let me have it." Instead of answering her, he took Shawn and put him in the small crib that had been set up by the bed. When Grady sat down beside her, he took her hand in his. "I'm afraid to know now."

"Winnie has had extensive work done on her body and face, I'm sure you're aware of that." She nodded, unsure now if she wanted to know what her sister had done. "Kurt—and he is positive that what he's found out is true, but he's looking deeper for you—he found that there was a huge insurance policy taken out on your mother just before she died."

"Yes, I knew that. But the policy was voided because Mom had stopped making payments on it in the months before she was killed." Grady only stared at her. "She did make the payments, didn't she? And Winnie somehow...she told me that there wasn't any policy and that was why she couldn't afford to raise me. She took it all. That's how she was able to finance getting her work done."

"Yes, but there's more if you're up to hearing it." Harper told him she wasn't sure. "I can understand that. Jake has lost his job, but not only that, your sister is no longer employable. What I mean by that is, she isn't going to get as many gigs as she had before, if any. They are investigating her for insurance fraud, as well as a couple of accidents on sets. Apparently, your sister does not like to be second banana to anyone."

"She hurt other models? Not that should surprise me. Winnie had to have the limelight or there would be hell to pay. It's mostly why I stayed away from the two of them. But she only lied to me about insurance. How is that going to get her into trouble with the company? That's what you're saying, right?" Grady shook his head. "I don't understand. She said that there wasn't any insurance so she didn't have to share it with me. I mean, that's terrible, but not something she should go to jail for, right?"

"There was a double indemnity on the insurance. It was added about six months before your mom was killed. Whatever happened to her, you and your sister were to share in the money, but with it being a murder, it doubled to nearly five million dollars. Winnie declared you unfit to handle the cash and made herself your guardian so that she'd have full access to the money. You were put in foster care not because she couldn't raise you, Harper, but because she didn't want you to take your share." She knew there was more and in her heart, she had a feeling she knew what he was going to tell her next. When Grady asked her if she wanted him to finish, she nodded. "Harper, Winnie had your mother killed. By Jake."

Her mind shut down. She wasn't sure how long she'd been out, but she looked around and found that somehow she'd been moved to another room or she'd wandered there. Shawn was in the little crib next to her, and Aisha was in the rocker knitting. As she moved back and forth, Harper tried to tell herself that it had all been a bad dream and Grady hadn't told her that her sister was a murderer.

"You all right?" She nodded at the older woman, then shook her head. "I would imagine that would be how I'd feel as well. Kurt, so you know, feels terrible for finding these things out for you."

"He didn't do it." Shawn...she needed him and bent to pick him up. "I know that it's supposed to be bad for them to be held all the time, but I need him. Just for a little bit."

She didn't want this woman to judge her, to think of her as incompetent. More than that, she really wanted Aisha to like her, as much as she seemed to like the other daughters-in-law. Holding Shawn to her, Harper wiped at her tears.

"You go on and hold him, my dear. I think you should do what feels good in your heart so long as it's not dangerous to either of you, and enjoy that little boy. There shouldn't be any rules for that part of loving your child." Holding him to her heart, Harper felt the tears fall harder. "Oh child, you're going to be all right. We'll make sure of it."

"My mother is dead because of my sister. She killed her for money." Aisha moved to the couch and sat down beside her. "I never really liked her...my sister was never nice. Not even when we were children. And I positively hated Jake from the moment I was introduced to him."

"He's being questioned about the things at the college soon. Also, his firm is looking deeper into some of the billing that he faked. I guess they're finding all sorts of things about him. I hated doing this to you, but that little prick was hurting you." Aisha pulled her to her shoulder and held her. "Change of subject. Jorden called here about an hour ago. He asked me to tell you that he has the studio set up for you. He even managed to find a couple of used kilns."

"He's such a nice man. I had it in my head he'd be a lot like Winnie because he's famous and all." Aisha said she beat that out of him at least twice a week. "I don't doubt that you would, either. But he's just a normal person, sort of embarrassed because he's doing so well."

"Jorden said the same thing about you just the other morning. He said he'd never met a more down to earth person, and he is so in awe of you." Harper snorted. "Yes, pretty much the same reaction I got from him when I pointed out he was just as well known."

"I love working with clay. It's so easy to shape and mold the way I want it." Harper handed Shawn to Aisha as she stood to pace. She was actually surprised at how wonderful she felt. "The first time I saw one of Jorden's paintings I was in a gallery that had asked to display my work. I remembered thinking, I'm in the same gallery with the amazing McCade. Then last night, while we were having dinner together, I watched him talk with his mouth full and spill tea down his front, like I do."

"Yes, I did try to raise all my sons to be better men, but they're basically all slobs." They both turned when someone laughed, and Harper smiled at Grady when he entered the room. "Here he is now, the slob of the hour. Grady, you have something on your shirt. Whatever is that?"

"Plaster. I was helping Kenton with a few things at the shelter. By the way, Mom, do you think you could keep an eye on Shawn for a couple of hours later? I'm to take Harper to the studio and show her around. Jorden wants to know her reaction, but he got called away."

"You know I would love that." Aisha asked when his next feeding was and Harper said she could feed him now. "You go ahead and do that, dear. While you're about that, I will go see the cook. I heard that he's made some of those wonderful scones again."

When they were alone, she looked at Grady. He was looking shy and all manly at the same time. Taking Shawn out of the crib again, she sat in the big rocker and started to feed him. He seemed to be an endless pit of hunger. As she nursed Shawn, she asked Grady about his shop. It was safe ground, she thought, suddenly very embarrassed around him.

"I open in the morning. We've sent out flyers and put an ad in the paper." He sat down on the couch. "Are you all right? Do you feel like going out?"

"I do. I want to see your brother's work too." Grady nodded. "Will you take me by your shop? I never got to go and help you that day, just watched as my sister was thrown out on her ass. Not that it wasn't entertaining, but I didn't see your new store, and I really want to."

"We can arrange that. Harper, will you go out with me? I know that sounds stupid, but we're married now with a child, and I just realized that I know next to nothing about you." She nodded, her emotions still on a pendulum all the time. "Good. I've made some arrangements to have Shawn watched. Kenton said he could have a bottle while we were gone if it was too late, and Mom said she'd give him a helping hand should he and Emma need it. I think he'll be all right, don't you?"

"Yes. He'll be just fine with them." She switched breasts, feeling pretty good about how much fun she was having, the first in a long while. "I don't want to talk about Winnie, Jake, or anything like that…is that okay?"

"Perfect." As soon as he left her, she felt the tears fall. She wasn't unhappy, she told Aisha when she came back with a plate of scones, but had only realized she'd fallen in love with Grady McCade.

"Good, because I believe he loves you as well."

Nodding, she watched Shawn nurse. She really did hope so.

CHAPTER 7

Ollie hated small towns. It seemed like everyone knew not only that you were a stranger, but where you were staying, the kind of car you drove, and what you'd had for breakfast. The little diner he was in, simply called Ma's, was no different than any of the other million and a half places he'd seen in his lifetime, either on the television or in real life. Nosey people looking for some gossip. He turned when the rest of the patrons did when the bell over the door danced a little song. It was like it was programmed into their heads to turn at the sound of the stupid thing.

These people, he knew immediately, were not from around here either. The woman looked like a fashion plate, the man a banker or attorney. They smelled of money, and snobbery was all over them, and for some reason, Ollie took an immediate and profound dislike to them both. As he sipped his coffee, actually really splendid coffee, he watched them find a place to sit. He was pretty sure he had the best one in the place.

Booth two had an unforgiving spring in the middle of the bench closest to him. The other one had an ass crease in it from the man who'd sat in it every day for the past ten years. Or so he'd been told. The next booth had one bench that was so-so and two chairs on the other side. Milly, the place's only waitress, had told him when he asked that Mr. Sheppard had come in one night a little on the sauced up side and had fallen against the table and the bench, breaking them all to heck. Her words, not his.

The bench in the corner held families, the one next to it as well. There were two other booths that had dirty dishes on them that hadn't been cleared as yet, and the one in the very back that was covered in office things. A computer, a calculator, which Ollie had been surprised they even made any more, as well as a schedule for this place. The manager would pop out every so often and work in the little spot, but mostly just socialized.

When the couple sat at the counter, a dubious place to say the least, neither of them seemed inclined to pick up the menu. Not that they'd have much to choose from. There was breakfast, lunch, and then dinner, all of them highlighted with a magic marker of varying shades of pink.

There were no choices to pick from; you just told Milly what meal you wanted and she'd bring you back whatever the cook deemed for it. He'd gotten hash browned potatoes, three eggs over easy, four strips of bacon, six thick pancakes, and gravy...sawmill gravy, he'd been told when he asked, and fresh sliced tomatoes. The man next to him in the booth with the broken seat, had gotten fewer pancakes, but he'd gotten ham and sausage with his bacon, and no tomatoes.

"I'd like some fresh squeezed orange juice, not the canned kind, and some wheat toast with no butter." Milly told her that they didn't have wheat bread, that the juice didn't come out of a can but a jug, and that the butter was on the side anyway. Ollie sipped his coffee again to hide his laughter at the expression on her face. "Do you have any fresh fruit?"

"Yeppers. We have some cantaloupe and grapes. I think maybe there is some 'nanners from last night's pie making, but I can check on that for you. Oh, and I believe there are some blueberries that I didn't use in the shake I made this morning. Really good too. I could bring you one of them." The woman declined but did take the fruit. "Whatcha want there, handsome?"

"Coffee and pancakes." She told him that all they had was breakfast. "I'm sorry. What? Pancakes were breakfast the last time I checked."

"You check on pancakes?" He nodded, then shook his head. "Are you right in the head, young man? I can bring you breakfast. Sometimes it has pancakes on it, most of the time anyway, but I can't be asking for them. Cook gets a might upset with us when we go making demands on him and his grill."

"I don't understand. I'll get pancakes if he wants me to have them? How the hell are you even a restaurant? You have to cater to the public, you know." Milly told him to watch his language. "Just give me breakfast. But I'm only going to pay for what I want off it, and not whatever you think to bring me."

"You sure are a snobby little thing, aren't you? And here I was thinking I'd have some fun with you later." She tore off the little slip she'd been writing on, something that Ollie didn't understand that she did. When she went to the window, instead of hanging the slip up, she simply yelled back that she had a fruit plate and a breakfast. She came by his table with a glass carafe of coffee. "How about some pie? We have 'nanner pie and some cherry. The 'nanner one is fresh, but if you want fresh cherry pie then you're going to be outta luck. It's just the frozen kind the cook makes when he feels like

111

it. I'm guessing he had a hankering for cherry and baked up about half a dozen of them."

He knew that she was making a point about the other couple. Laughing, he told her that he would only like a refill on his cup. She gave him another small pitcher of milk, not cream because it was too costly, and his bill.

Ollie was amazed that the place could stay in business with how little they charged for their meals. Breakfast was five bucks, lunch was six, and dinner was eight. Pie, if they had it, was two dollars; ice cream, which Milly told him was a stable—not a staple, but a stable—was only seventy-five cents, and coffee was free so long as you ate some food with it. Ollie had been eating here since he'd arrived in town. Mostly for the entertainment value, but he also liked the food.

He was paying his check when the man's breakfast was set before him. He'd gotten his pancakes, all right. It looked like he had a dozen or so of them. There was also a thick slab of ham, and potatoes that Ollie knew were delicious, at least half a dozen eggs all pretty in a row, as well as sausage links and patties, and a large bowl of gravy. Then Milly set a basket of the still warm biscuits next to the plate, with a jar of marmalade and one of honey. The woman's plate of fruit not only had the aforementioned 'nanners, but blueberries, strawberries, kiwi, cherries, and cantaloupe. There was also a pretty muffin still steaming from the oven, as well as a crock of butter.

"I can't eat all this." Milly told her she didn't have to; she wasn't her momma to make her eat her plate clean. "What I mean is, this is too much food. You can't possibly think that someone like me would eat all this. And look what he has. Jake cannot have this either."

The man apparently thought differently as he was digging

into the meal like he'd been starved for a month. He'd already polished off one of the biscuits, as well as two eggs. He told the woman, with a mouth full of food, that it was the best he'd had in ages.

Ollie left them to their meal. Whatever they were in town for, he'd bet the man would be here for each of his meals from now on, even if he had to leave the woman at wherever they were staying. It wasn't until he was out on the sidewalk that he noticed their car. More importantly, their license plate.

They were from the same state as his jewelry. Ollie walked behind the car, snapped a picture of their plate with his camera, and made his way to the pay phone that was about a block from where he was standing. He waited while his contact at the police station gave him not only the name of the owner of the car, but an address as well. Then he told him who they were.

"They're the people that are suing your girl." He asked him for what. "I don't know. All my paperwork says is it's for breach of contract. Close to two hundred grand now with penalties. Oh, and the woman you asked me about? She's married to one of the McCades. Their marriage license was filed a couple of days ago."

"What about the baby? Any mention of it?" He said not that he could see, but that didn't mean there wasn't one. "I've seen her; she's going to have it soon if not already. I wonder if these two are here to collect on their bill or something more. You don't think they've found out about the jewelry, do you?"

He'd never told anyone what the jewelry was worth or what it was supposed to do once it was all together. Ollie didn't believe in that shit, so it mattered little to him what someone else believed. All he cared about, ever, was the money and how much he could get. This guy, like the very few others that he might call upon for information beyond his abilities, thought it was from a robbery long ago that had been committed against Ollie's father.

"Nah, I think they're just trying to get in touch with the sister. They've run into some trouble of their own, but I'm not finding much out about that part. He's lost his job at some stuck up place, and she's in retirement from hers, whatever the fuck that means. She's a cover model, it looks like. Maybe she's losing her looks and they cut her lose. Don't know, don't care." He thanked him for his help. "Oh, before I forget, there was another piece of your shit found. It's in Florida, of all places. I got a guy going down to verify but not touch, just like you said."

"Good job. Let me know what you find out." He saw a man standing near the car he'd been using and told his contact he'd call him back. But before he could do much more than look both ways before crossing, the man was standing in front of him.

"I think I warned you." He backed away from the guy from the plane and nearly tripped over his own feet. "You have been sticking your nose in things that are none of your concern again, Ollie. Did you not think I'd make good on my promise?"

"I've not done a damned thing to any of them." He only stood there, his arms crossed over his chest. "What do you think you're going to do to me, huh? People know where I am. They're going to miss me if you pull me from this place."

"No one cares where you are. There is no one that will miss you. And even if there was, they'd not make any kind of effort to find out what happened to you. And I think I might have mentioned this before, no one will find you anyway should they bother to look." Ollie moved back when the man moved closer. "You will keep away from the jewelry and the McCades, or so help me, the next time I see you, you'll be a dead man."

Almost as soon as he finished the sentence, the man was gone. Just like in the plane. Ollie leaned against the wall for support, fearful that whoever the bastard was, he'd return to do just what he said.

When he was able to walk without trembling, Ollie made his way to his car. Glancing into the diner, he saw that the woman was gone but the man was still sitting on the stool. He appeared to be enjoying a cup of coffee. If these two were related to the woman that had his jewelry, then perhaps he'd just found his ticket. But he had to be careful. That fucker pretending to be a vamp wasn't going to catch him unaware again.

CHAPTER 8

Grady wasn't sure what to do with his hands. Did he hold hers? Did he help her out of the car? He knew what his mom had taught him about women and how to treat them. He was just unsure what to do with a wife who just had a baby and they were on their first date. He smiled when he thought of how dumb that sounded.

"You all right?" He said he was, just thinking. "I'm a little nervous. I know that Shawn will be all right, but I've never had a baby before and I'm not sure what I should be feeling. I feel guilty, if you want to know the truth, for not being with him all the time."

"Mom said she'd call if they needed you. I don't think they'll have any trouble, but she said they'd send pictures too, just so you'd know they're watching him. As for feeling guilty, believe it or not, I feel the same way. Like I'm falling down in my duties as his dad. Silly, because we're going to be good parents, but that doesn't lessen the feelings." He opened the door to the building that Jorden had been working in over the last few months. "Jorden said not to expect too much. He did get you some used equipment, and there is clay left from when he was working in it. Also, he said it would be as simple as making a few calls to get whatever it is you might need. He is really excited about you possibly working with him."

"I have some pieces that I want to bring here, if you think that's all right." He told her it would be wonderful. "Jorden told me that he's going to use the lower part of the building for.... Oh Grady, it's wonderful!"

The entire bottom floor of the large warehouse had been cleaned out and redone. The walls were painted a nice neutral color, the windows all replaced and shiny now with long drapes that hung from the ceiling to the floor. And the hardwood floors on this level had been sanded and polished to a lovely shine. Every time one of them found a large piece of furniture or a stand to set things on, they'd bring it to Jorden to be used as a prop. Jorden had set things around the open space with some of his pieces on them, while others were waiting for things that Harper brought in.

They walked around the room, her telling him what she could see on the piece and him nodding. The dragon, Caelin, spoke to him just as they were moving to the back of the room and near the stairs.

You have not shown her your dragon as yet, have you? He told him he'd been a little busy. *Yes, I'm sure that you have. I have a desire to see the new child soon. I hope that he will enjoy the gift I have given him.*

Gift? Caelin asked him if he'd show her the dragon. *I'm not sure she's ready for that. I mean, I'm not even sure I'm ready for it.*

She will enjoy it. I have had a peek into her mind, and she is excited to see him as well, but is scared of asking so as not to offend you. Grady asked why that would offend him. *You will need to ask her that. Emotions are very foreign to me. Much like the thought process of the female mind.*

Grady wasn't sure even most women knew their own

mind. But instead of asking her about that, he pulled her into his arms and stood holding her. It was a wonderful feeling having her so close to him. But he enjoyed having her hold him back more. He ran his finger over the torques at her arm.

"Caelin said that you want to see the dragon I have in me." Harper looked up at him. "I've never shifted before. I'm not even sure what mine looks like. The others, my brothers', they're all different in colors, but there is a shade of blue in each of them. Kenton's has blue eyes. Jorden's has blue wings. I'm not sure what I'll have."

"Show me." He nodded, but didn't let her go just yet. "I'm sort of afraid myself. I mean, is he huge? Does he have sharp spikes along his back? I've wanted to see him, but am afraid you'll be terrifying too."

Stepping back from her, Grady tried to think how to make this work. Caelin laughed a little and told him to think of him, just his dragon. Closing his eyes, he thought of the dragon for only a moment, seeing him there just before his body felt like it had been pulled through a wringer on the old washer his grandma had.

"Grady?" He opened his eyes and looked down at Harper. He was taller than he was before, he could feel that. Afraid to move, he stood as still as he could when she moved toward him. "You should see you. Oh my God, Grady, you're beautiful. Can I touch you?"

Yes. He knew that she heard him…for whatever reason they had a stronger connection now. Grady thought of kissing her, something that he'd only been able to do at the wedding. But when her fingers moved over his body, he felt as if she were caressing him all over. *I can feel that. It's not so much a touch as it feels like a vibration against my body.*

"Your scales are blue. Not just a regular blue, but cobalt.

And they're glossy, like a high fire glaze that is almost blue black. But I think it's your eyes that are the most gorgeous. They're almost clear, with your scales giving them a hint of color. Do you know what the inside of a shell looks like? That's what I'm thinking." She moved around him and he had to be careful not to stretch out his tail. He wanted to, but didn't want to hurt her if he didn't have much control over it. "You have wings. Can you spread them out too?"

Of their own accord they came out. He felt lighter for the moment. He flapped them once, just to see how it felt, and his body lifted with it. When Harper was in front of him again, he moved slowly down to her level and touched his head to hers.

"My arm kind of burns where the torques are. And I have the strangest need to have you nip me there. Like bite me in the arm." He licked his tongue over her arm and moaned at the flavor of her. "Do it again, Grady. I need to come, and that's going to bring me."

He moved his head to her arm, touching his nose to the mark there that to him, in this form, glowed. Touching his tongue to her again, he heard her cry out, felt her fingers dig into his arm when she screamed out his name. And when she cried out a second time, this time for him to bite her, he gently sank his teeth into her skin and tasted blood.

He felt it. Everything about her seemed to race over his mind. Her emotions. Her fears. Grady tasted her memories, even ones from her childhood. The first bottle she took. The touch of her mother's fingers over her cheek. Her daddy's tears when he told her he had to leave. His voice telling her that he wasn't meant to be a good man. Grady heard her dreams that woke her in the middle of the night. Her fear of being abandoned, and when that happened how alone she'd felt. He knew how deeply her sister's treatment of her had made her feel. Even the foster family that she lived with and the trouble she had there. He had it all, knew everything there was to know about her.

Pulling her to him, careful not to hurt her, he wrapped her in his wings, held her head to his heart so that she could know that it beat only for her. Her heart was his, her mind an open book, her body his haven.

When she pulled away, looking up at him, he watched her eyes. He saw the way something moved through them. It took him a moment to realize what it was, and it was then that he saw the dragon, in flight in a darkened sky. And the rider upon his back.

Hello, my loves. The voice was not that of the dragon, but of a woman. She spoke to them both, Grady thought, and for some odd reason, he wasn't afraid of her or of anything she might try to do to them. *It has been a long while, but you have freed me.*

"Who are you?" He wanted to ask himself, to know who the beautiful woman was he could see as well as he could Harper. She sat upon the ground in front of a large deteriorating castle, flags flying in the breeze, and he saw blue dragons on a gray background on them. Harper continued before he could ask her where she was. "I know you, don't I? I've seen you... in my dreams. When I first touched the jewelry."

"Yes, that was I. I had no idea when I cast this spell to keep you all safe that I'd be a part of the necklace. I was, at one time, the center clasp, I believe. Then after we were separated, Warrior and I, I lost touch with him as he was within the necklace. I am the queen, the first McCade dragon ever born. My dragon companion, Warrior I called him, is within the largest blue diamond ever seen. His spark, the one that I put there, is the being that speaks to you even now. But we were

121

parted when my husband, the crazed king, decided that since I'd have no sons for him I was unworthy, and tossed me aside for another." Grady told her what he knew of the other pieces. "He is still lost then, the largest spark of him?"

"We've been searching for all the pieces and have yet to find the necklace. I think we will soon. But we talk to a dragon; Caelin, he has called himself. He has been guiding us and the women that touch the pieces here, to my family." She smiled at that, and Grady could see her sorrow as well. "I don't think he knows of you. He seems childlike in his knowledge of even the simplest of things."

"Yes, he would. Warrior was a brilliant dragon, and would do what I wanted with the slightest of touches. But he, like me, has been trapped for many years, and we have lost touch with the way things have become. When I took Warrior's sparks from him, hiding them away in each piece of the jewelry that he'd forged for me, more of his memories were taken as well. When he was weak from the loss of it, I sat upon his back just as my husband, the bastard king of my land, came through the castle doors. He wished me dead so that he might marry a woman who would bear him children, a son he hoped. It never came to pass with this woman, nor any other that he took to his bed." Grady asked her how she was related to them if there was no son. "Oh, but I had his child. A son that he knew nothing about, had no idea that there was any from our horrific union. My son's name was Caelin, just as the warrior you have now is called. I had given him my magic when he was but a child. I taught him to hide and fight better than any man so that he'd be safe. Even when he was little, he understood the importance of keeping strong and out of harm's way. And when he was old enough, he killed his father for what he had done to myself and the world he'd come to lose, the kingdom and all its riches."

She moved closer to them...Grady could almost touch her. And when he felt his body shift, his dragon moved back to himself and he became a man again. The queen stood before him and Grady dropped to his knee.

"Stand and look to me, my child." He did as she asked, and then helped Harper stand when she asked for her to look at her as well. Harper, too, had bent before the woman, and he wondered about that and realized it was because of how she presented herself, as the queen that she was.

As they stood there, the queen looked him over. Grady hoped that she'd find him to be a worthy man for some reason. His dragon moved along his skin, not painfully or out of fear, but to let him know he was there for him, for them all.

"You look how I have dreamed my son to. You have his eyes now. The blue of the oceans. I should like to touch you now, if you please." He saw her sorrow then, the tears that she shed for her long lost son.

Grady bent to her. He was a head taller than her, bigger everywhere, and it made him nervous that she was so tiny. The moment her fingers touched his cheek, he felt the warmth of her love and it reminded him of his own mother. Then she moved to Harper.

"Don't harm her." He had no idea why he spoke to her that way. The queen hadn't harmed him, but he wanted her to know that Harper was his to protect and he would, no matter who she was. "She's my mate. And the mother of my son."

"Yes, your son. I have met him as well, but only from my position on the other side. He will grow to be a great man, this child of your heart. You will have other sons as well, and a daughter. In my time, many more years than I care to think about, daughters were of no use. I think I should like to see her one day. She will be a woman of great happiness to countless many people." The queen turned to Harper again. "You have braved so much, my child. Given more than most would have in the same circumstances. You are a great warrior yourself. I should ask you a favor. A small one, but a favor all the same should you not wish to do so."

~~~

Harper looked at Grady, then to the woman again. A favor? So much could be lost or gained in a favor, she knew this. But for whatever reason, Harper thought a favor for this woman would be better for her than for the queen.

"Yes. Whatever you wish, I am at your command." The woman nodded and kissed her on the cheek. The power of it, the magic feeling that swept over her, had her staggering slightly. Holding onto Grady, Harper asked her what she'd done.

"You did not ask questions of my favor. You had your reservations about it, fear that I'd harm you. Yet you said that you'd help me. A gift such as that, one of undying trust, should be rewarded, don't you think?" Harper wasn't sure and said so. "Such a delight. Now for the favor. Your daughter, would you name her for me?"

"I don't know your name." The queen laughed and said that she'd not shared it as yet, but she would. "All right. I'll name her for you. So long as you don't care if it's a middle name or first. I won't have her bullied because her name is odd. All right?"

"Yes. I like that. You have made provisions for your child that you know nothing of. Yes, I care not where you put it, but that her name is like mine. I believe you will not find it so overly vexing for her. 'Tis served me well all my life." Harper thanked her. "My name is Nordic in origin, but no less powerful for it. I am Prisane Justalyne Harper McCade, Queen of the Dragons and High Grand Witch of all my lands." Harper looked at Grady to see if he had caught this. Harper? Her name was Harper too? "I can see that you're confused. As am I, if you wish the truth. My family name was Harper. So when I was old enough to take a name that I would wear proudly, it was a name that I used. It is my honor to have you called the same."

"I can use that. All of it, if you don't mind." Grady nodded his approval and she smiled at Prisane. "Do I call you queen? Or my lady? I'm not sure.

"You may call me Prisane if you wish. Or grandmother. I am that and more." She looked at Grady. "You have much to do, to learn, before you travel to your kingdoms, young Grady. I would like to help you along with that."

"That would be.... Wait, did you say my kingdoms? I don't own a kingdom. I have a house, a nice one that my sister in-law sold me. Too cheaply, but I...I don't have a kingdom." Prisane told him that he did now. "It should be for the family. I mean, we're all going to share in this magic, it should be for the family to travel to and keep."

"They will have their share of the riches. There is more than plenty to spread around. But, as you have awakened me, you shall have the castle. I'm afraid that it's in poor shape at the moment, but you can fix it up. And it will be better for your touch." Prisane turned to her. "You will fill it with children, I think. Many offspring that will run the halls as my son was never able to. Yes, you will have such fun there. And you need not worry about funding. I have made sure that you have plenty for that as well."

"Wait. I think something is wrong here. This castle...I'm not worthy of something so grand. Falling apart or not, it's too much." Harper turned to Grady when the queen did. "My brother, Kenton, he's the oldest. He should get this castle. Don't you think? I mean, he's like this kingie guy anyway. Bossy and all." His face turned red. "I'm sorry. I'm slightly overwhelmed right now."

Harper reached for Grady's hand, as he had hers whenever she was feeling like a deer in headlights, and knew that it calmed him as it did her. As they stood there, before a queen older than the building they were in, she felt comforted by her presence. Stronger for her trust in them, and more importantly, Harper felt like she could take on the world and come out on top.

"You will need the knowledge to go on from here, I think. The ability to see things that no other will know. A gift, or a curse you might think it, that I have used my entire life. You both will need magic, a great deal of it, to keep the family safe, and the children born to it out of harm's way. I should like to pass it to you." Grady asked what of the others. "You will share what you have. Both of you will. No harm will come to the babes yet to be born, but it will enhance them. However, you both will have the greatest part of it. You will have my all."

"All?" Prisane nodded. "All as in you won't be around to use it too, or just all because you're sharing it?"

"My all. I cannot stay here, my child. Should I do that then there will be more trouble than you can imagine. This trouble with your sister, and the man that pursues you even now? It is nothing, not a drop in the seas, for the trouble that would befall the McCades should I stay, projecting my magic like a beacon to them." Her smile was sad and it tore at Harper's heart. "When you have your girl child, she will bring me back. Not as a person, but in spirit and magic. Her magic, like that you will pass to her, will keep the future generations safe. The dragons as well. And there will be more. Dragons will come to you once they set it all together. May I touch you now?"

Harper nodded and put out her hand. She wasn't sure what Prisane needed to touch of her to give her the magic, but she figured that she'd show them. As soon as her hand was wrapped around hers, Harper held tighter to Grady's and knew that he was feeling it too.

Power. It radiated from the touch of the queen to her heart and mind. As memories and information flooded her head, she felt herself grow stronger as the queen weakened. The dragon too, the one in Grady, was there…Harper could see him. And when she was released from the magic that surged over her, Harper staggered back and closed her eyes. As she was falling back, her only thought was that she loved Grady.

When she woke she was lying on a soft blanket. Grady was standing near the window of the studio. He turned to look at her when she sat up, and she told him she was fine when he asked.

"I'm better than fine. I feel fantastic." He grinned at her and she smiled. "I wanted to tell you something. I love you."

"I love you as well. With all that I am. I'm so very glad that you're in my life, in my heart." He pulled her up from the blanket and into his arms. It was a place that she thought she could gladly spend the rest of her life. "Prisane is gone. I can feel her, like she's right on the edge of my mind, but she's not here anymore."

"I know. I feel her too." Harper wrapped her arms around Grady. "What do we do now? I'm assuming that there is something we should be doing."

"I have no idea." They both laughed. "I was playing around with my dragon while you rested. He's stronger.

Bigger too than before. Not that I knew anything about him, but I know that he's different for me. And then there is this."

He stepped back from her and she waited while he unbuttoned his shirt. She felt her mouth water then dry up as he pulled it off. As he stood before her, his chest smooth and his muscles tight, Harper curled her hands into a ball and put them behind her back so she'd not rub him. He said her name when she just stood there.

"I'm looking, but...." Then she saw it. The dragon was on his arm. Not a small one either. He seemed to start at his shoulder then curl around his arm to his wrist. "Does he move?"

When he didn't answer her, she looked at him. There was a look there, one that she wasn't sure what it meant. Was he terrified? Sickened? But when he smiled and nodded she asked him to show her.

"I'm not entirely sure how I do it, but if I put my arms together like this, he moves from one to the other." He showed her, the dragon moving down his right arm to his left. "And then I can move him to here."

The dragon moved from his arm to his chest. As he sat up, stretching out his wings and curling his tail around him, Harper felt something move over her own arms and pulled up her sleeve. She stared at the smaller one on her arm.

"Grady?" He took her hand in his, and she held him tightly. "I have a dragon. And it's moving. On my arm."

"I can see that." He pulled her hand to his chest, the one where the dragon curled around her. As hers began to move, she knew it was somehow going to join his and jerked her hand away.

"I'm not ready for that yet." He just nodded. "Grady, we have dragons on our persons. We talked with a long dead queen, and we have a castle. I don't know that I'll ever be ready for this. Just...can you just show me the art room? I mean, I'm really trying hard not to freak out, so show me something normal. I need normal."

He didn't laugh at her. She was sure that if things were reversed she might have. Or maybe not. But he took her to the elevator, one of the old fashioned kinds that was gilded and had a crank to choose a floor, and took her to the third level.

"The second level is going to be used for setting up the art. Jorden needed a place that he could put together canvas. Frame things when he had them done. Also, a shipping area. The upper levels, three and four, are for the two of you." As he told her about what the building would hold for them, she let her mind drift over the fact that they had dragons. Her life had surely taken a strange turn, she thought.

CHAPTER 9

Aisha moved her cart to the next aisle. The shop was crowded today, at least for a Monday she thought, but she knew that someone was following her. The man that had been dogging her for the last hour and a half wasn't anyone she knew, but she had a feeling that he knew just who she was. As she leaned down to pull another little outfit off the shelf, she nearly screamed when Kurt suddenly appeared.

"He can't see me. Nothing will happen to you, my lady, but I should like for you to pretend that I'm not here." She pulled out her cell phone, looked at it, then put it to her ear and winked at him. Kurt laughed. "I think I know just where your boys got their smarts. You are a brilliant lady."

"Hello, my friend. And of course I am. Now, tell me what you know and I'll go on with my shopping. I have a new grandson that you must come and see." He told her that he'd seen him just that morning. "Good for you. I got to sit for him yesterday. Most fun I've had in a while. So tell me, my dear. What is going on with you?"

"The man following you has it in his head that should he take you, the others, your sons, will gladly give him what he wants. Namely the jewels. I don't think he realizes that they're attached to the women, do you?" She asked Kurt what was

131

going to happen. "If you'd not mind, and I will make sure that you are unharmed, I should like for him to try to take you. It will go a long way in having a reason for me to murder him."

"I hate that it should come to that. You're a nice young man." Kurt told her that he was much older than her. "No matter. I think of you as one of my sons. And I hate that you must resort to murder to end the world of such a person. To me, you're a nice young man for taking care of this old lady."

"Thank you. You were always my favorite McCade." She laughed when he did. "The man's name is Ollie Morrison. Earlier this month he killed two people. I'm sure there are many more, but one of them was simply an innocent, the other a man that was after the same thing he was. His crime is yet unsolved, but I have spoken to Dalton and I think he'll be able to finally close the case. He is a brilliant officer too, and I should like to see him promoted."

"Good luck with that one. I've been trying the same without much success." She picked up a little jumper and held it up to cover her mouth while she continued in a much lower tone. "The baby needs to be safe, you know that. All of them do, but he is too small to call out to us should someone come for him."

"It's the man's plan to take him if this should not work out with you." She looked at Kurt, stunned that someone would take a small child. "Aisha, you know that I cannot lie to you, but if this man does get the child, any of the children, he will kill them. He's done so before to get what he wants."

"Then we'll go with your first plan." He nodded at her and she put the jumper in her cart. "I have some shopping left to do. Do you think I have time for it?"

"It would be better if you did. He plans to take you when you return to your car. He will never get you, but he will try."

Putting her phone in her purse again, she moved between the shelves now, not seeing what was there. "Aisha, the baby needs things, you came here to get them. I promise you, Ollie will never touch you. And Shawn will be a well-dressed little man."

Nodding, she reached blindly for the first thing she could touch. But when she held it up before her, just to have something to hide her tears, she burst out laughing. Then turning it in a way that Kurt could see it, he laughed as well.

"I will pay for these things, all of them, should you do me the honor of getting them. This will be the perfect gift for young Shawn." Nodding, she looked for more of the bedding set that matched the blanket that she'd found. She and Kurt had so much fun gathering the beautifully made things with the blue dragon on it.

They ended up buying a changing table, all the bedding, including the blanket that she found, as well as clothing. Not just newborn things, but clothing that he could grow into. And at the rate he was growing, it wouldn't be long before he was wearing the bigger items.

There was a diaper holder, wipe warmer, as well as receiving blankets, quilts, and even a few outfits. When a clerk came by to ask if she needed help, Aisha told her of her new grandson and the things that she'd found, and the young woman took her to yet another part of the department and showed her that there were bottles, pacifiers, and other dragon items to go with the set.

By the time she made her way to the checkout, Aisha had completely forgotten about Ollie and his plans. But when she saw him just outside the door, she paused after having her things bagged up. Kurt told her she was safe, but she didn't feel it; her good mood was soured by what was going to happen next.

Going out to her car, she was loading the things in there, still a little excited about showing Grady and Harper what she'd found. As she put the last bit in the trunk, the stroller that had dragons on it as well, she felt rather than saw the man coming up behind her. Turning at the last minute, she knew that she'd startled him, but she didn't move when he pointed the gun at her.

"I want you to get in your car and stay there until I get in the other side. And if you so much as make a belching sound, I'm going to shoot you where you stand." Aisha huffed at him. "My dear, I'm not in the best of moods right now. I've never known a person to spend so much time in an infant department before."

"I'll have you know that I do not belch, as you so rudely put it. And should I do so, it would be followed quickly by pardoning myself. You, sir, are bad-mannered if you think otherwise. Why on earth would my shopping habits have you pointing a weapon at me?" She backed him up with a finger to his chest. "I have a grandson now, a wonderfully amazing little boy that I have enjoyed buying for. And now here you are messing that up for me. What do you think you're going to gain from this?"

"All the riches in the world. Get in the car, please. I have appointments to keep, and you are just the first of many things I must take care of." Aisha thought about fighting him…she could have she knew, but she might get hurt. Kurt told her to just get into the car and she'd be fine.

Doing as he said, she got into the driver's side and waited. Before she could do much more than put her belt on, Ollie was gone. She started to get out to see what happened, but Kurt, through their connection, told her to go on home and then tell Kenton and the others what occurred.

But I don't know what occurred. He laughed. *This is not a time for you to be humorous, Kurt. I don't want you hurt any more than I would like me to be. What did you do with my would-be kidnapper?*

He is resting, lying in a field not far from here. I have only beaten him a little, broken one or two ribs, and rendered him unconscious. Of course, he does lie in a pile of cow manure for a warm pillow, but I thought that fitting for talking to you about such a horrid thing as belching. And there is a large bull eyeing him now; for what, I'm sure I don't want to know, but should he walk funny in the morn, 'twill be laughable, I think. The man, not the bull, with the odd walk.

They both laughed, her for the image that popped in her head, and Kurt.... Well, she was sure that it might be considered bad form to be having so much fun at someone's bad luck, but the man, Ollie, had brought it on himself.

Whatever am I going to do with you, Kurt? He asked her if she'd just love him. *Well, of course I can. I already do, as a matter of fact. You're a good boy. And friend.*

Thank you, my lady, as are you. If you would be so kind as to call in your sons, starting with Dalton, I think we can safely say that they'll take care that you have no more unwanted visitors while shopping. She asked him where he was going. *I have this and that to do. I have purchased a home nearby. I've decided that I cannot live without my little dragons.*

Good. I'd very much like to see you more. Maybe you can find a mate and I can have little vampire grandchildren to play with. She could almost feel his sadness. *I am so sorry, Kurt. I have been careless with my words. I wish with all my heart that your Sophie was here with you now.*

As do I, my lady, as do I. Now, call your sons, we have things to do today. And I, for one, am looking forward to holding that little grandson of yours.

As she pulled out her phone, much too sad to reach out to her sons, she thought about how none of them had contacted her through this ordeal. Then Kurt told her that he'd planned it that way, so they'd not come charging in and ruin his plans. She asked him what his plan was.

To show the monster for what he is.

Aisha shivered. She would not like to be in that man's boots when her boys found out. The women either, for that matter. She so loved her growing family. When Dalton answered, she smiled when he sounded a little harassed.

"Dalton, I'm at the mall and some man tried to get me to go with him at gunpoint." That should shake them up, she thought, and laughed when he started cursing. "Yes, I feel the same way. Can you come here? Also, if you'd be so kind, you could help with some of the heavier items I was unable to get into my car."

~~~

Ollie limped through the bed and breakfast and knew that something was off. He wasn't sure what it was at the moment, but he had a feeling that he was going to find out sooner rather than later. After the night then morning he'd had, there was little that could have surprised him. Having to hose himself off had been a nightmare, and he'd had to toss out one of his most prized suits. Someone, he thought he knew who, was going to pay for this.

Taking a right instead of the left that would have led him into the dining room, he stood stock still in the kitchen where four men — large ones — were standing and having a cup of something. The one looking at him not only offered him a cup of what turned out to be tea, but also a scone. Ollie took both and sat down before he knew what the fuck was going on. Two more men walked into the room, and he had a feeling

136

that had he gone to the dining room those men would have brought him here.

"Ollie, you have been a very busy boy, haven't you?" He looked at the man speaking and said nothing. "Kurt tells me that you were warned, several times, to stay away from my family. What the hell possessed you to try and kidnap our mother?"

"I haven't any idea what you're talking about. I've only been in town for a few days, and I haven't met your mother, or you for that matter." He wanted to stand and leave them there, thought that perhaps it might save him a great deal more pain, but he had a feeling he'd get no further than his feet under him before they took him down again. "What makes you think I even know who your mother is?"

"Oh, I guess we should have introduced ourselves. I'm Kenton McCade, and these are my brothers. I think you might have come here under the assumption that my brother Grady's wife, Harper, might have something you think you should have." He looked at the man he'd seen with the woman but hadn't realized they'd been married. "So now that you know who we are, you can tell us why you were going to harm our mother."

"I didn't touch her." Not that he hadn't planned on it, he'd just never gotten the chance. Someone, and he an idea who that might have been, drugged and dumped him in a field. "She was shopping where I was and I saw her go to her car. If something happened to her, then you've got the wrong man." He started to stand but his body hurt too badly for any quick movements. "Now, if you gentlemen will excuse me, I have things to do."

"Kurt said to tell you that he warned you as well." Ollie turned to them then. "Also, he wanted us to tell you that the piece in Florida, it's been taken care of. As has the man that went there to get it for you. By the way, it wasn't a part of the set. We know where they all are now."

"You lie." The man that had introduced himself as Kenton said that he wasn't. "There is no way you know where the pieces are. They're as elusive as anything in the world. I should know, I've been looking for decades."

"And killing people that got in your way." There was no point in denying it. He had a business to run. "What were you going to pay the man you were going to have kill us? A million, a billion? How much was it going to be worth to you to kill six women and their mates?"

"More than you can see in several lifetimes. And I will get them all too. I have the right resources and money to back them up." Kenton only shook his head. "You have no idea what you're fucking with right now. I will have my jewels, Kenton, and once I do, you will die not having any of it."

"They're not for you to take. Not that you're going to live long enough to collect on them anyway." Kenton sat down at the table with him, and the five other men leaned against the stove and other things in the room, looking casual. Ollie knew it was an illusion; he also knew that they'd never kill him. These were not men to get their hands dirty.

"People know where I am." Kenton told him he'd said that before to Kurt. "And Kurt would be who? The man who has altered his mouth to scare little girls? I'm a grown man, as you are. You can't possibly believe there are vampires in the world."

"I do. I know a few of them. And yes, Kurt is a vampire. Just as we're dragons." Ollie laughed and told him to get real. "You don't believe me? Well, I'm just going to have to show you then, aren't I? But not right now. I'd like to talk to you about why you came for our mother."

"I tell you what, you give me all the pieces of jewels and I won't bother your family again. Better yet, give me the locations of the rest of them too, and I will pay you ten million dollars and leave you alone. I think that's a great deal, don't you?" Kenton shook his head. "No? Well then, I guess you're going to have to keep looking over your shoulder. I'm not giving up."

"I think, then, that you'll have to die."

Ollie laughed. These people would not kill him. As he thought before, they were not the killer types. The simple fact that they had come here to talk, instead of doing what he would have done and just killed, showed what sort of people they were.

They took him outside. The backyard of the B&B was lovely this time of morning, and he commented on the deer that were in the yard, and the flowers that surrounded the wide board fence. Just as he was ready to ask them what this was about, a wolf about the size of a Saint Bernard came into the yard as well, startling the deer off.

"Nice. Just when you think it's just too pretty to be real, something like that happens. You guys don't have a gun, do you? I mean, we could get rid of the wolf population right now." Ollie laughed and then stilled when four more of the large canines came into the yard. Then more and more until there were at least three dozen. "You think we should run?"

"Run? If you want to give them a thrill, then you go for it." The second brother — Grady, he thought his name was — stood in front of him. "Something we've discovered lately is that when we shift, we get to keep our clothing. Might not seem like a lot to you, but it was to us. We shared that little trait with the local pack."

When Grady nodded to the wolf, Ollie fell back on his ass when as a whole they became men. Not just men, he saw now, but men and women. And there were more than he'd first thought too. There had to be about a hundred of them, most of them humans, the others still wolf.

"This isn't funny." Kenton laughed with his brothers. "What the fuck are you pulling here? You know as well as I that this is all done with mirrors."

"Is it? Well, I'd like for you to take my hand." Ollie jerked from Grady when he took his smaller hand into his. "What? Are you afraid now? Did we scare you a little? And here I thought we were going to have some fun."

Grabbing the man's hand was a mistake. He knew that the moment that their palms touched. Something, he had no idea what, rolled over him. Then Grady was gone and Ollie was holding hands with the scariest thing he'd ever encountered.

"My brother wants me to tell you what he's saying. I wish I was the one holding your hand, but he won the coin toss so you have him and not me. It might have been easier on you had it been my hand, but I guess we'll never know. But we kind of wanted him to do it too, because we've not had the pleasure of seeing his dragon. Impressive, don't you think?" Ollie nodded. "All right. Grady, the dragon here, he wants you to know that you have three choices. I'd be hard pressed to pick which one I wanted, but he's letting you decide."

"How are you doing this?" Kenton asked him what he meant. "This isn't real. There are no such things as dragons, shifters, and the like."

"Really? I guess you holding the hand of a dragon and seeing a pack of wolves here wasn't enough. Okay, let me think...." Ollie wanted to hit the man. He was much too calm and thought he was funny. Ollie did not appreciate him or his humor in this. "I got it. How about if Grady here burns you to a crisp?"

"Are you fucking nuts? No, I don't want him to burn me at all. What the fuck is wrong with you people? Are there mirrors around here? Is that how you're doing this?" The smell of something burning had him look at his arm. His suit coat was on fire, the flames of it jumping high on his arm to his face. Just as he was going to run for the nearest water, one of the other brothers hit him with a towel, knocking the flames out. "You fucking burned me."

"No, he didn't burn you at all. He did, however, burn your suit. I don't think he's very sorry about that, even though he asked me to tell you he was." Ollie looked at him, then at the dragon. There was blood now on his hand and wrist where he was being held.

"I'm going to call the cops." One of the brothers moved to the front and said they were here. His name badge said McCade. "I want you to arrest these men. They're trying to kill me."

"I think you should be more worried about the pack. They can smell blood." Ollie turned to the pack and saw that they had shifted back to wolves and moved closer to him. Jerking again on the hand that the dragon held, he felt the tear in his skin, the blood running down his arm, and the front wolf snarled at him. "That's Ralph. He's the new pack alpha. In the event you don't know what that means, he's in charge. And on his order, you'll be dead."

"I'm not going to stand here and listen to this shit. Let me the fuck go." Kenton asked if he was going to leave them alone. "Are you willing to come to my terms? Give me the location, as well as the pieces you have? If not, then no, I'm not leaving here empty handed."

141

"I'm not going to do any of those things, and I think you know it. So that brings us back to your three choices. Dragon, wolf, or vampire." He asked him what he meant by that. "Do you wish to die by dragon, which means death by fire; wolf, who will tear you apart piece by piece—which I will say, it probably won't be quick; or vampire. Kurt will tear your throat out. It might be quicker, but I don't think it would be any less painful. What's it going to be?"

Ollie stared at them. They could not think he was going to make any sort of choice like this. Not to mention, did they really expect him to believe this was what they were actually going to do? Apparently.

Ollie looked at the wolves, all of them lying on the ground except the biggest one. The dragon no longer held his hand, but Ollie knew that should he run they'd sic the wolves on him. There wasn't anyone here that resembled a vampire, and he thought perhaps they hadn't thought that far ahead. Kurt, or whatever that guy's name was, probably had to have more dental work done to look that good.

"All right, I'll play along. You want me to pick my demise. This is the stupidest thing I've ever been a part of, just so you know." He looked at the pack, the dragon, and the men. He wasn't afraid of them. It was a tactic, a poor one, but he really didn't blame them for trying to scare him. "So this vampire, he's not here. Am I to assume that you have to take me to him?"

"No, Kurt is here. He's just in the shadows. He's a vampire, you know, and can't withstand direct sunlight for long periods of time. Would you like to see him?" Ollie said no, he had enough going on. It was funny really. These people had to learn follow through. Once he picked, what the hell did they think they were going to do to back it up?

"I'm thinking that the vampire might be my best bet. He's probably hungry anyway." Kenton said he never thought to ask. "Things you have to do, Kenton...may I call you that? Anyway, when you make a threat, especially to someone that is as well-known as me, you need to be able to back things up. Like this pack. Did you really think I'd believe they'd attack me? Not likely. And this dragon. I'm not sure how you did this...it's impressive as fuck, but not all that convincing. You need to work on your delivery too. You just don't have it."

"I'll remember that. So you've picked Kurt to kill you?" Ollie laughed and nodded. "All right."

They turned and walked away. Ollie laughed harder then. They were such amateurs at this. He might have enjoyed teaching them a thing or two if he wasn't going to—

The wind rushed his face. Ollie might have fallen; he wasn't sure, but he was flat on his back. Trying to sit up, he wasn't able to. Looking down at his body, he could see chains at his wrists and ankles. Ollie called out, his mind blank on how he'd gotten here.

"Hello, Ollie. I told you I'd be back." The man standing over him was huge, his eyes dark. Then he realized they weren't dark, but red and glowing. As he leaned to him Ollie tried his best to shrink away, but his hand was at his throat, nails dug deep into his skin. "I'm going to enjoy this a great deal more than I thought."

The pain was too much, sickening and powerful. He screamed over and over as he was torn up. Nails, long and sharp, entered his belly. His intestines were pulled free, then shown to him. Ollie felt his arms break; his legs were snapped. All the while, through it all, Kurt explained to him what he was doing, how he was hurting him, and begging him to scream more.

"Come now, you can do better than that. Scream for me. The blood is so much richer for it." Ollie did scream, louder with each new pain. Kurt laughed at him, made fun of how his balls were so small, even holding them up for him to see after removing them. And when he leaned to his throat and said it was time, Ollie begged him to end him. To take away the pain.

"Do you now believe, Ollie Herman Morrison? Believe that there are dragons, wolves, and vampires?" If he answered, he had no idea. Teeth tore into his throat and he felt his blood flow from the wound. Ollie did believe, but it was much too late for him to say so.

CHAPTER 10

Winnie read over the paperwork twice before she tossed it to the table. She and Jake had been staying in this little hotel room for three days now, and she was sick to death of it. It was beneath her. And now this bullshit. Who had found out this crap?

And that was all it was too. Just water under the bridge now. Who cared if her mother died and left them both the money? Harper hadn't had any use for it, not like she did. Not only that, but Winnie had made something of herself. What had Harper done? Nothing. She taught a little bit at some school, not even good enough to have a full time job.

When Jake came back—from the diner, no doubt—she asked him about the envelope that had been laying on the little table this morning. He said he'd not put it there.

"Jake, you had to have. I didn't. Who else would have come in here, put it right there with mine and your names on it, and left again? It had to be you. And if not, someone just came in here, laid it out, and didn't take our wallet or purse." He sat on the room's only chair and picked up the envelope. "There is no reason for you to read that. I'm speaking to you."

"It has both our names on it, not just yours." Of late, just since they arrived here, they'd been arguing a lot more. Before all this, they would just be upset like civilized people, but keep it to themselves. She didn't care for his tone, nor the way he was constantly picking fights with her. "It says that we're being sued by Harper, for the insurance money that your mother left her and you. How did she find that out?"

"I'm assuming…." She snatched the paper from him. "I'm assuming that she found some sucker that is a great deal smarter than her and he looked. I'm sure it's because they figured out that we're related. I told her not to tell people that we were sisters. It's going to ruin my career for people to know that. Me? An award winning model, attached to a lazy person who is knocked up without a husband."

"She has one. They were married a few days ago. And I guess she's had that brat too." She asked him how he knew that. "This is a small town; everyone knows everyone's business. It's all they can talk about. How this Grady person has a new wife and they have themselves a little boy. It's my little boy, Winnie, and now some other person is out there that knows about it. You told me when we started this crap that it would never come out. This will hurt my chances at being a partner, if I can ever get back to work. And so you know, I'm blaming that on you as well. Christ, this is so fucked up."

"I'm sure that he has no idea who the father is. Perhaps he thinks it's his." He asked her how that was supposed to work. "I don't know, Jake. She's pretty stupid, and I can't imagine that she'd find herself anyone smarter than her. She can't even find a good job."

"Yeah, I think you're wrong about that. Did you know that there is this guy here, Jorden…? I don't remember his last name, but he's opening this large studio, and he's asked your sister to join him in it. He's a painter or something." Winnie asked him if it was Jorden McCade. "That sounds right. Hey,

146

isn't that the doctor's name that you had all set up to give you the baby?"

"It is. And I want to know why he didn't tell me. Christ, this is a major fuck up. Not only is that brat out there, but my sister has it in her head that I'm going to somehow pay her back for the insurance that she didn't even deserve." She sat down and wanted to cry. "Jake, I can't get anyone to call me back about working. I've even called people that I would otherwise never consider. No one is taking me on. I just don't know what to do. I've become perfect, and now I can't get anyone to take my picture."

"I've been out looking for jobs as well. It's like there is an email that is telling every firm around that they're not to hire me." She asked him what they were going to do. "I don't have any idea. Not a single clue. The firm called to ask where they could send my things. I was hoping they were calling to say they'd made a mistake, but that's all they said. I'm sorry, honey. I didn't want to tell you because you were so depressed and it was too much for me. Also, I guess this explains why I couldn't pay for my breakfast…our accounts are all frozen. When your sister applied for us to repay her plus interest, it must have frozen our accounts, so we're broke except for any cash we have on us."

"How can she do that to us? This is so unfair of her." Jake nodded. "I knew that we should have dumped her in another country instead of putting her in foster care. Now all this is coming back to make us look bad. I won't have it, Jake. She is going to have to stop this right now. How am I supposed to work if she's spreading these things about me?"

"What if someone digs deep enough and figures out everything, Winnie? We could go to jail for a long time if they do. And I might not ever be able to work for a firm again." She told him he didn't like it anyway. "No, but I was getting pretty good at pretending that I liked it. Also, my firm is looking into my overbilling. I might have to pay that back too. Harper is going to make it tough on us. We need to take care of her now, and not wait on the money coming. She's going to ruin us."

"I agree; this shit has got to end. This is all Harper's fault. Every bit of it. All she had to do was what I told her and none of this would be coming out. Damn it all." Winnie started pacing the room. "Once I get her to retract this nonsense about the insurance stuff and get rid of that kid, we can salvage things. She'll *have* to pay us back now. And I think we should consider selling the baby now instead of just giving it to someone to get rid of. A little boy on the market might bring enough to get us back home and the down payment on the new house."

"Do you even know how to do that?" Winnie asked him if he did. "No. But I know that there are all kinds of people out there that will buy a white kid. Christ, to think that I have this part of me out there just moving through life like it has a right to. We should have just killed Harper too when we did your mother."

"I hadn't had time to fill out any kind of insurance forms yet. Besides, I think it would have looked bad had anyone cared enough to check." She continued pacing. "How much cash do you have on you? I mean all of it, Jake. No holding back on this."

"I have about sixty bucks." She looked at him, shocked. "I told you that I was buying a couple of suits. I can't believe I have three suits that would have cost me half of one back home. And they even tailored them to fit me. What do you have on you?"

"Why the hell didn't you use your credit cards? I know you have them." He told her that the firm cut those off, and again about the bank freezing their personal accounts. And besides, they didn't take cards in the shop. "I cannot wait to get back home. This place is a dump, and everyone here is hokey."

She wasn't sure if that was true or not. Winnie had only left the room once a day since being here. Jake usually brought her food from the diner and she'd eat it right there. But yesterday she noticed that she'd put on three pounds. That would not do. When she went back to work, and she would, she wasn't going to have anyone making fun of her. So now she had a bag of carrot sticks, not organic like she wanted, and water. She thought by the time she went back to modeling she'd be at her peak weight.

The phone ringing startled them both. Neither of them had a working cell phone. She, unlike Jake, still carried hers around with her. It wasn't good for her image to not have a cell, so she'd take it out on occasion just to show people she wasn't poor. She'd walked up and down the sidewalk twice to bring a little culture to these people. Not that she thought any of them noticed.

Winnie answered the phone when Jake didn't appear to understand he should have. "Hello?" There were noises in the background. It sounded like a dog that had been wounded or something. She was ready to tell whoever called to just kill it, but they spoke first.

"Winnie? It's Harper. I wanted to talk to you about a few things." Winnie told her she had things to say to her as well. "I'm sure you do, but this meeting is mine, not yours, so you'll listen or I hang up."

"How dare you think to talk to me that way? You have no right to say anything harsh to me...I'm your sister." Harper laughed and Winnie felt her temper skyrocket. "Harper, I want you to pay us what you owe and give me that kid. I know you had him."

"I did. He's wonderful too. You should see him. Dark hair like mine. The cutest little button nose. You can hold him if you want." Winnie told her no way. "Your loss. Especially since he's your nephew. But that's not what I want to talk to you about. It's about this bullshit that you've brought to my door. I want you to meet me at the diner in one hour."

"And you just expect me to drop everything and do as you say? It doesn't work that way, Harper. I'm the injured party here. You'll do as I say." Harper said nothing. "There, I'm glad to see that you understand. Bring a certified check with the full amount of what you owe me for your room and board at the clinic, and the kid. I want this finished so I can return to work. Also, this stupidity about the insurance. I have no idea where you might have picked up that information, but I won't have it marring my reputation. You will cease that as well. After that, I'm leaving this dump once and for all, with that brat. People are waiting on me."

"No, they're not, and we both know that. You're finished as a model. You couldn't get work in a porn movie unless I said so. You lied, cheated, and hurt me. I'm done playing by your rules." Winnie asked her what she was talking about. "Mom's death. I know what you and Jake did."

Winnie sat down. "You don't...I have no idea what you're talking about. Mom was killed by being in the wrong place at the wrong time. You know that."

"What I know is that you had Jake kill her. How could you do such a thing, Winnie? She was our mother." Winnie said nothing, but shared the phone with Jake when he moved close enough to hear. "You'll be at the diner in one hour, or I'll make what I've done to you so far look like nothing. Do you hear me? Oh, and since I know that Jake is listening in on this too, you should bring him as well. There are a lot of people with questions about his behavior as well."

When the line went dead, Winnie carefully put the receiver in the cradle. She was moving very slowly, making sure that she didn't let her temper take control of her. There wasn't time, she knew, to redo her makeup and nails before this sham of a meeting with her deadbeat sister. Winnie looked at Jake and cleared her throat before speaking.

"We have to end this. Today. She's gotten out of control and I want her gone. Once we take care of her and that kid, we can get back to our lives again." He asked her what she had in mind. "You have that gun still? The one that we took care of Mom with?"

"Yes. We decided that if we kept it, then no one could find it to use against us. You thinking to kill her and the baby?" She nodded. "All right, but after this, we're going away. For a long time. I'm too stressed to even think."

"All right. We'll get that money from her first, kill them both, and move on. No one will care about her, and I need this finished." He asked her how they were going to kill her sister. "I don't know. This diner, it's busy. Maybe that's why she picked it. Or because they have all that fattening food. You know how she didn't watch what she ate. I think we can get it done in the back of the place. Leave her in the dumpster like we should have in the first place."

"I can do that. I'm over this crap anyway. I hated my job and being a lawyer, but the pay was good. We really need some money." She promised him they'd have it by the end of the day. "Good. I'm glad. I feel better already just knowing this is about to end, Winnie. I miss our life. It was perfect. We're perfect."

"We are." As she walked to the little bathroom and refreshed her makeup and hair, she thought of her sister. What a loser she'd turned out to be. Nothing at all like her. Successful and beautiful. "Perfect. I'm perfect."

~~~

Harper looked at the little bassinet. Her son should be in it; they should be out having a wonderful time today. But instead she was meeting her sister and ending a longstanding feud that she was sick of. The doll that was bundled up in the little blanket showed her how little trust she had in Winnie. She was startled when Jasmine sat down across from her.

"Hey there." Harper smiled at her. "You do know that this is going to turn out just fine, right? That no one but your sister and her husband are going to get what they deserve?"

"What is it you think is going to happen?" Harper knew; right down to the very detail. As did Grady. "Do you think that she might, oh I don't know, come in here and tell me that she's sorry? That she's been a bitch to me all her life and that was horrible of her?"

"No. And I'm pretty sure you don't either." Harper looked at the doll when Jasmine did. "You know that this has to end with her, right? That you can't be dealing with her crap and having a wonderful life with Grady."

"I know that. It doesn't make it any easier to understand why she did all this, but I know." She looked at Jasmine and knew that of all the people in the world, she could trust her and the rest of the McCades with anything. "When we met up with the queen, she gave us this weird ability to see things in the future. Some of them are fuzzy, but we can."

She wasn't sure she was going to believe her. Jasmine, of the two new sisters that she had, was the one that she depended on most. Not just because she already had a child, but because she seemed to have her life in order somehow more than her and Emma did.

"I don't want to know." She started to tell her that she could tell her everything she wanted. "No, I don't want to know my future. I think.... Maybe it would be safer for me to know, but it would also be crippling, I think. I can see myself being dependent on asking you if I should leave the house. Should I go to this sale to buy things? Maybe you'd tell me that I'm going to die in childbirth and I'd fret so much over that, I'm sure I'd not function for the child. No. I just don't want to know."

"You don't die in childbirth. I want you to know that because I can also feel your fear of it now." Jasmine nodded. "I'm afraid. Not just of this freaky thing we can do, but of what happens today."

"You know? Do you live?" Harper nodded. "Then do just exactly what you need to do to make sure that happens. You have a family now, a huge one, and it's growing larger by the day. Make sure at the end of this, you go home to us. All right?"

"Yes. But can I ask you one thing? Just a small favor?" Jasmine hesitated, but in the end she nodded. "Don't go to the tag sale on Fourth this week."

"Bad?" Harper nodded. "All right. But don't make a habit of that. I don't want anything to happen to you, but I don't want to die either."

"You won't. Just don't go."

After Jasmine left, with the promise that she'd not go to the sale, Harper pulled out her notepad and began sketching out designs that she was going to work on in the studio. The place was set up nicely. She loved that she was going to be working with someone as famous as Jorden. Harper smiled when she thought of how Jorden felt the same way about her.

Yesterday she'd gone to see Kenton too, to ask him about sex. She had been so embarrassed about it, telling him how she felt and the changes in her body since she'd seen the queen. Harper had a feeling, however, that the way she knew she was ready for sex had to do with the bite that Grady had given her when he'd been a dragon.

"You've only just given birth about two weeks ago." Harper explained to him that there was no more bleeding, she wasn't sore, nor did she feel like she'd done anything extraordinary at all. "I understand that. Emma, she cut her hand the other day. Not badly, but enough to require stitches. But when I returned with my bag to put them in, not only was the wound healed, but she didn't even have a scar. I think whatever the queen gave you, it's being shared with the rest of us. So, if you feel good enough to have sex, then I would say go for it. I'm sure Grady won't mind either."

She'd planned last night to rock Grady's world, but the shop opened tomorrow and he'd worked really late in getting things ready. By the time he'd returned home, she'd been sound asleep with Shawn in the bassinet right next to her.

Harper looked up from her drawing to look around the room. There were a lot of police here, she knew. As well as an FBI agent, an attorney that had volunteered to come and monitor things, and Kenton, who was with Grady in the kitchen. They were the only ones that were well hidden. The rest were waiting on the customers and pretending that this was a normal day for them. Then she saw Jake and Winnie coming down the sidewalk.

Her sister was as perfect as ever. Not a single blemish on her body that she could see, her hair just like she'd seen it on pages in magazines. Harper knew that it was all fake, from her perfect lips all the way down to her dainty little ankles and toes. It had amazed her to find out that her sister had had work done on her entire body. She wondered what she'd look like today had she just left herself alone. Jake, however, looked like a man who was facing a firing squad. An odd combination, for sure.

He looked...Harper thought he looked like he was deranged. His face was set in a sort of pained look. He'd put on some weight, as much as twenty pounds since she'd seen him last. Also, and Harper wasn't sure, but he looked like a man heavily into drugs. Closing her eyes for just a moment, she knew then that her worst fears were confirmed. He was high, he did have a gun, and he was planning on using it on not just her and the baby, but anyone who got in his way. People were going to die today, and it saddened her so much.

As soon as they sat down across from her, Harper let out a long slow breath to deal with them. When Shelly, one of the policewomen that worked with Dalton, came to take their order, Winnie ordered water with lemon, but Jake ordered breakfast, just as Harper had.

"Look at you. So you decided to have some work done, did you? You look better. Not pretty, you'll never be that, but at least I'd not be ashamed to be seen with you now. And I see you've lost weight. The brat, I'm guessing." She told her sister she was happy and in love, that was all. "Love? Entirely overrated, if you ask me. Not to mention, you cannot have me believe that happiness would do that to you. I'm happy and I don't glow. No, I think it's either work done on you or you've been taking some drug."

"No, no drugs. I'll leave that to Jake." Her sister looked shocked, then she looked at Jake, who was trying to straighten up. "I would like to ask you some questions about Mom and

155

what you did—"

"Are you seriously going to bring that up now? Christ, Harper, she's dead. Get over it. And I know you found out about the insurance thing. That should have gone to me anyway. I used it to better myself. I'm positive that is what Mom would have wanted. Besides, one of us had to make something of ourselves. You certainly didn't." Harper said nothing. Her sister would believe what she wanted no matter how much she tried to tell her otherwise. "Did you bring a check? Not a personal one either. You'd better have a certified check made out to cash. I just don't trust that you wouldn't cancel payment on it and I'd be stuck with that as well."

"I'm not going to pay you anything for what you did to me. And I'm not finished talking about what you did to Mom. You and Jake killed her for the money." Winnie slammed her hand down on the table, not just making Jake jump, but making the salt and pepper shakers turn over too. "Your temper means nothing to me. And you can't expect me to pay you for the things you've done to me. Not to mention, I think you taking my half of the insurance money from Mom more than covers whatever you have in your head that I owe you. Now, back to Mom and the murder of—"

"Harper, you're really pissing me off. I have no idea why that money still bothers you. Knowing you, it wouldn't have done a damned thing for you other than to make you fatter. And I did nothing other than put you in a nice facility that took better care of you than you ever did. So what if those people that got you were less than nice? You're still alive, aren't you? And as for Mom, I will not have you bringing that up again. It's over. She's gone, and you and I are going to come to terms with how much you owe me and nothing else." She asked her about the baby. "I'm glad you brought that up. I'm taking him when I leave too. And you're not going to do a damned thing about that either. You've fucked me over enough, and I'm going to sell him to the highest bidder on the black market."

"No you're not. He's my son." Winnie waved her off. "You're not leaving here with my child, Winnie. I didn't want to have one, but now that he's here, I want him with all my heart."

"Really? You think you're just going to talk to me like this? Well I have news for you, baby sister, Jake has a gun. And if you don't cooperate, then I'm going to have him use it on you. We're taking that kid and you'll keep your mouth shut, and for the first time in your miserable life, you're going to do just what I tell you." Harper said nothing. "All you had to do was just get rid of it when I told you. Christ, it's not like you have any money to raise it. And I'm sure that new husband of yours is just as much a lazy bastard as you are."

"Actually, I have a great deal of money. So does he. We have a castle that we're renovating, a home that is much bigger than anything you've been trying to buy, and a family support system that…well, let's face it, one like you never were." She smiled as she picked up the doll. "My son and I are going to live here, happily and without you hanging around."

The gun appeared in Jake's hand. He didn't wave it around, but simply aimed at her and fired. The impact of it hitting her in the chest, just where she'd put the doll, was sickening and painful. The aching of it—she knew it was a couple of broken ribs—made her breath hitch. But when she was thrown to the seat, her entire body covered by one of the officers, Harper laid very still. Without looking, she knew just what had happened.

CHAPTER 11

Grady watched them process the scene. The entire diner had become one. There was blood on the windows behind where Jake had sat, and some had spilled out onto the floor surrounding the seat where his wife had been. Grady tightened his arms around Harper as he held her.

"I'm all right, you know." He said that he did, but he needed to hold her. "I think you putting all that sand in the doll is what saved me from worse pain. I mean, a broken rib is small in comparison to what it could have been."

"You're not helping." She giggled. "I can't believe she did this. Either of them. I know that we saw it, but I still find it hard to accept as reality that they actually did it."

When she pulled back from him, he let her. He didn't let her go—Grady wasn't sure he was ready for that just yet—but he did look down at her face. Wiping away the tears that he could see there, he told her he was sorry.

"Jake is dead, my sister isn't going to make it either, and now here I stand feeling relieved that it's finally over. I feel... Grady, I feel horrible." He pulled her back into his arms and held her while she sobbed. "My sister wanted to kill me."

Kenton came to stand in front of them and said nothing. He shook his head and Grady knew that Winnie hadn't made

159

it. Jake had ended her life and the police had ended his, before they could harm anyone else. The thought of what might have been made Grady shiver.

When Harper was released to go home, he took her. Mom had been asked to watch Shawn…mostly to keep her safe as well. They'd all been afraid that their mom would have leapt in front of the gun just to save her family. But her being with Shawn had eased Harper's mind too.

"He's such a good little boy." Grady wasn't surprised when she didn't ask how things had gone. He was sure that one of his brothers would have told her. "I've given him his bottle and put him in the nursery. If you don't mind, I think I'll just stay here tonight. Keep an eye on him for you two. You look exhausted."

Harper was exhausted. And when he picked her up to carry her to their room, she didn't protest. As he laid her on the bed, he started to leave her when she grabbed his hand. Pulling it to his mouth, he kissed it.

"I love you. So very much." He told her that he loved her too. "Grady, don't leave me. I don't think I could survive if you did."

"I'm not going anywhere, love. I promise you." When her hand fell from his, he kissed her gently on the forehead and left her to rest. Going downstairs, he saw his mom waiting for him. "She's asleep. I think she needed this today."

"Of course she did. I'm sure that no one wanted them dead, but she did need to face her demons. That girl wasn't right." He nodded. "Grady, they said that had you not put sand in that doll that Harper would have died as well."

"I know that." She nodded. "Mom, are you all right with this? I know that you really didn't have any choice in the power that we shared, but you're okay with it, aren't you?"

"I think so. I do get a little startled by it at times. Like just yesterday. I was shopping for things for the house when I touched this woman. Poor thing was on her last dollar and trying her best to figure out what to take home for her daughters to eat. I cannot imagine being that poor." He asked her what she'd done for the woman. "Oh, this and that. Carmichael's was having a contest; did you know that? I had no idea, but she was their one millionth customer and won a five-hundred-dollar gift card, as well as a full cart of food. By the way, son, she'll be by in the morning to help you at the shop. First day opening and all, I thought you could use the assistance."

Grady just laughed. Christ, he had the best mom in the world. He hugged her tightly before following her into the kitchen for some late dinner. Kurt was in there with Rachel and Walker, telling them about the house he'd just purchased.

"I don't think it's going to be too hard for me to renovate. I have spoken to the new contractors in town and they're going to do things the way I want them." Grady nodded as Rachel made him a sandwich, as well as one for Kurt. "There are some pieces that I have in storage that I need to bring over. And others that I want to get rid of. You think Jasmine will take them?"

"I'm sure she will, but she'll make you take the money if she sells them. She's pretty set on that." Kurt only nodded, not saying he would take the cash. "I need for you to do something for me, if you don't mind."

"Anything, you know that." Grady nodded but didn't know how to tell his friend what he knew. "Grady, if this is about the power you have, I don't want to know anything. I've been around for a very long time, longer than most vampires I know. If I'm going to die, then so be it."

161

"She's coming here. Your mate, she's coming." Grady watched him take a bite of his sandwich, then laughed when he started choking on it. "Yeah, I thought that would get you."

"You can't be serious. I've.... My mate is gone, Grady. You know that. Sophie died a very long time ago." Grady nodded as he took a healthy bite of his own sandwich. "You're fuc... you're lying to me."

They both looked at his mom when she laughed. Kurt could curse better than anyone he'd ever known, stringing together words that most people had never heard of. In several languages as a matter of fact. But around his mom, he tried his best to curb that part of himself.

"I would never lie to you about something like this. But I swear to you, she's coming here." Kurt stood, then sat again. "Would you like to know who?"

"Yes. No. I have no idea. But I can't have another mate. We have one. I told you that." Grady waited for him to come to a decision as he ate the rest of his dinner. "No. I don't want to know. If you say she's coming here, that means she's not here yet. I have a chance to...I don't know, but I can decide whether or not to run. I should. I don't want to.... She's really coming?"

"Yes." When someone knocked at the back door, Grady didn't move. Kurt started using his nice vocabulary then... he had figured out what Grady had been saying. She was literally coming here.

"You fucker." Mom hit him in the back of the head. "Aisha, she's here. What am I supposed to do with a mate? I'm older than she is, set in my ways. Not to mention, I've had my chance at happiness once. We don't get a second. What am I to do?"

"Apparently you are getting that chance. Now, I would

start with opening the door and not cursing at her like a madman. Go on, open the door for her." Kurt glared at Grady as he made his way to the door. When he opened it, Grady had to lean over in his seat to get a look at her. Christ, she was beautiful, and not alone. "Oh my. It's the woman from the store. Opal Gray."

Grady got up and moved Kurt out of the way when he just stood there. Inviting Opal in with her two little girls, he asked her to have a seat. The children held onto their mom as they stared, terrified, at Kurt.

You're scaring the kids, Kurt. Kurt looked at him when he spoke. *Kurt, you're scaring them. Pull yourself together or this isn't going to end well.*

As Kurt did as instructed, Grady introduced himself to her. His mom told him that she'd forgotten about inviting her here this evening to meet him until she had shown up.

"I'm sorry. I don't have a sitter, so I'm not sure this will work out with me helping you. I have a nice room now that I'm staying in, but I don't care for the people—"

"You'll stay with me." She looked at Kurt when he shouted at them about staying. "I mean, I have a home, a large one, that you can stay in. With the children. There are nine bedrooms in the place, more than I can—"

"You're very kind, but I can't stay with you. I don't know you." Kurt nodded but sat down now. He was trying hard not to order Opal around, and Grady could see that it was costing him. "Anyway, Mr. McCade. I know that I said I'd work for you and all, but finding someone I can trust with the girls is difficult right now."

"I have two sisters-in-law that can help you out. Both of them are going to have babies, so I'm sure that they'll jump at the chance to get some practice. And my wife has a son too,

163

a newborn, so she might help out as well." Opal was already shaking her head when Harper came into the room. "This is my wife. Harper, I'd like for you to meet Opal and her two daughters."

"Hello." Harper got down on her knees before the little girls and smiled at them. "I have a little boy; would you like to meet him?"

The youngest shook her head until the older nodded. As they talked quietly, Grady looked at Kurt. The man was suffering in the worst kind of way. Not only did he look like he was terrified out of his mind, but he was hungry for the woman too. When Harper stood, the little girls followed her, each of them taking her hand as they left.

"Now, as you can see, we're a trustworthy bunch. And I can really use your help tomorrow." She still wasn't sure and kept glancing at Kurt. "He's harmless as well. A little overwhelmed at the moment, but harmless."

She leaned to him and whispered. "He's not human. I mean, I already figured out that you're not either, but he's a vampire."

"Yes, I am." She turned and looked at Kurt. Grady could see the fire in her eyes when she told him it was rude to listen in on private conversations. "Since you know that I'm a vampire, you must also know that I can hear a pin drop in the next room. Would you like to know what your daughters, lovely children by the way, are saying to Harper?"

"No. Are they being rude or something?" He told her no, they were very well behaved. "I raised them all by myself, but I think I did a good job of it. What are they saying?"

"Mostly that they're happy to have met Aisha. That it was nice having food in their belly until they were full. And the older one, I believe her name is Chris?" Opal nodded. "She's hoping that you move into my home and stay there, because she's terrified that someone at the shelter is going to tell your ex-husband where you are and he'll come for all of you."

"He's dead." Kurt nodded. "I mean, I didn't do it, but I'm not sad that he's gone. He wasn't good to us. Especially when Cindy wasn't a boy like he said I should have had."

Grady left them there as they worked out the arrangement for them moving into Kurt's home. Kurt hadn't used compulsion on her, not that he could have, but Opal was afraid of the men in the shelter. All men as a matter of fact. Grady found the girls, all three of them, in the living room watching television with his son. Grady thought life was pretty much perfect.

~~~

Harper hadn't ever tried to be sexy. She wasn't even sure that she knew what to do with her body. She had lost some weight, a great deal of it after the baby had been born, but she didn't have a good feeling about herself. Especially naked.

The nightie that she'd gotten yesterday was pretty. Sexy too, she thought. It had taken her almost an hour to buy it. Not that she was busy picking one out, but getting up the nerve to take it to the counter and actually pay for it. Now here she stood in their bathroom, thinking that she'd done something incredibly stupid. Harper tried to think what Emma would do.

Yes? Harper was startled by the voice, but went with it when she realized it was indeed Emma. She told her what she was doing. *Ah, so you're going to finally consummate your marriage. Good for you. What's the issue?*

I got this sexy thing…well, I think it's sexy. I've never thought of myself that way, so this is all new for me. Emma laughed and she felt embarrassed. *I'm not sure how I got you, but I'm really sorry. I should —*

No, don't. I'm sorry. I was trying to think how on this earth you don't think you're sexy. I mean, I'm into men, but I think you're incredibly beautiful, and while I don't know sexy for women, Kenton says that you're pretty. She asked Emma if she told Kenton what they were talking about. *No. I'd never do that to you. But he has mentioned how you almost glow now. Ever since you had Shawn, you sort of radiate this kind of mystic kind of beauty. So, where is Grady while you're hiding in the bathroom?*

He's still at the shop. There are some last minute things he needed to get done before tomorrow. I don't know why I'm doing this. Emma told her because she loved Grady. *I do, but I'm not exactly a model.*

She thought of her sister and that she'd been so beautiful on the outside, but ugly on the inside. And that she was dead. Her big sister had tried to kill her, and now she was dead. She felt sorrow through her entire body, and had to hang onto the sink with it. Emma said her name several times before she could answer her.

I'm all right. Just overwhelmed at the moment. Emma said she would be as well and was still talking to her when she cut her off. *I don't know what I'm supposed to feel right now. I mean, my sister is dead, and all I can think of is that she's not there to harm me again. She tried to kill me, Emma.*

I'm not trying to compare my life with yours, so please don't take it like that, but I had the same thing happen to me. Not just my brother, but my mom and grandfather. Of course he saved my life, but it was still so depressing to think that someone wants you dead, someone you thought should love you. When Bart...he set up a bomb to go off in a building I was in. Just like I was nothing at all. So how did I feel...? Well, betrayed mostly. And like you, relieved. But mostly I felt like I could move on, be my own person and live.

Living is the best thing you can do, I think, when something like this happens. And even though you didn't care for the tactics that she employed, you have a part of her that you can love like she never did you.

I forget sometimes, now that Grady is here as well as the rest of you, that he's not his father...that Grady is only going to be his stepfather. Emma said she was sure that Grady didn't feel like that way. *No, he doesn't act like it. I mean, he tells everyone he's his son, and you should see his face when someone says he looks like him. Like he's invented having children or something.*

That's our Grady. He's the best. She laughed with Emma. *I'm sorry for your loss, Harper. For all of them. But mostly, I can't help being happy that she's gone and not you. I love you like you're my own sister.* Harper thanked her. *I think that whatever you picked out for Grady will be amazing. But I'm telling you right now that he won't care one bit if you're wearing a sack or silk, so long as you're happy.*

After telling Emma that she was fine now, she decided to take a long bath and relax. Stripping down while the water ran, she thought of the diner and what had happened. Things that had led to the death of the two people in the world who had hurt her the most. Jake and Winnie.

Jake had had a gun. And when he'd pulled it out of his pocket, things went from simple conversation to all out terror in just a few ticks on a clock. Then her sister's words finally got through her mudded head.

"We're going to take that kid and you're going to keep your mouth shut, and for the first time in your miserable life, you're going to do just what I tell you." Harper had said nothing; she hadn't been sure what she could have said at that moment. "All you had to do was just get rid of it when I told you. Christ, it's not like you have any money to raise it. And

I'm sure that new husband of yours is just as much a lazy bastard as you are."

The gun had gone off then, hitting what they both had thought was the baby. Just like that, Jake had pulled a gun and shot his child. Then almost as if he knew what he'd done, or perhaps it had been in his head all along, he turned the gun on Winnie and fired once before turning the gun on himself. By then, however, the police had fired too, killing Jake before he could kill himself.

Even though she'd been thrown to the seat, her body covered by one of the undercover officers that had been sitting in the next booth, she could hear her sister. Her last breaths, as it turned out, were wet sounding. Blood pooled in her lap, and from her position on the seat across from her, Harper knew that Winnie wasn't going to make it…the bullet had gone right into her throat and out the other side.

They were both dead, and for what? She'd been asking herself that question for the last few hours. Winnie had had it all. Even a husband that seemed to be a great deal like her. Not necessarily in a good way, but they did have a lot in common in how they felt that everyone owed them and they were above things like laws that didn't suit their needs. They had money, fame, as well as a good home life, and friends. Not as many as Harper had thought, but a great many people had called asking after her sister. She was sure a lot of them were just seeking answers that the newspaper hadn't given them. Or the news. But for the most part, people were sorry for her loss and said they'd keep her in their thoughts.

Harper had been notified by Jake's firm that he had an insurance policy they were still trying to work out the details on. Kenton had the family attorney call them, and he was going to make sure she got it soon. There was also one on her sister. Both she and Grady had decided the money would be put aside for their children to use.

She heard the door open to their bedroom just as she was pulling the nightie over her head again. Harper told Grady that she'd be out soon, and he said he was tired. Hoping that she wasn't making a mistake, she moved out of the bathroom and into the bedroom just as he was pulling his shirt over his head. He stared at her for several minutes, long enough for her to feel that she wasn't turning him on as she had hoped.

"I wasn't sure when you'd be home." He nodded and Harper wanted to turn and reach for a towel or blanket to cover herself up with. "Did you get everything—?"

"Turn around for me." She did as he asked, trying her best not to cry. When she was facing him again, he smiled at her. "You have no idea how many times I've thought about you naked. Or nearly so, as you are right now."

"I talked to Kenton. He said I was fit." Grady tossed his shirt to the chair and she watched as it slid to the floor slowly. When Grady said her name, she looked at him. "I've never done this before. I mean, I've had sex, but it was just something to do. That sounds horrible, like I make it a hobby to go around having sex. I don't—"

"Harper." She snapped her mouth closed. "You're beautiful. Sexy. And you're all mine."

"I am. Forever." He moved then, his body sort of gliding to her, and she took a step in his direction. When they were only a few inches apart, Harper did something that she'd wanted to do since she'd met him; she ran her hands over his chest to his navel. "You're very firm."

"I am extremely firm, and needy." He put his hand over hers and moved it down to his cock. "You have had me in a state of firmness since I first laid eyes on you."

"I'd like to undress you." He dropped his hand from hers and took a step back. "I'm sort of nervous, if you want to know the truth. I've never...I guess you could say this is a night of firsts for me. I've never made love as a wife. Never undressed a man before. And I even bought a nightie, something I've never thought I'd wear. I wanted to please you."

"You have. All the time, every day of our lives." Harper felt her heart beating harder in her chest as she moved her fingers over his ribs to the button on his pants. "I'm going to try really hard not to rush you, but I've wanted you badly for a while now, so don't be surprised if I take over."

"I don't mind. I'm in love with you, Grady McCade." He kissed her then, a hungry yet gentle meeting of mouths and lips that made her breath catch. "Now, let me try to seduce you. Just don't laugh if I make a mistake."

"Never. And seduce away, love. I'm here for you." She nodded and put her hands on his button again. Pushing it through the hole, Harper was determined to make him sweat a little first.

CHAPTER 12

Grady held his breath as she worked on seducing him. He could smell her…every part of her body was aroused, and he wanted to toss her onto the bed and take her…he needed her that much. Just when he thought he couldn't take any more, she laid her head on his chest and cried.

"I don't know what I'm doing." He lifted her chin up so that he could see her tear stained face. "I have no idea how to make you want me. How to be sexy. I'm just me, and I'm a failure at even that."

"Do you have any idea how much I love you?" She nodded and smiled at him. "All right, but do you know how difficult it's been for me to just stand here, let you touch me, when all I want to do is take you? Christ, woman, if you were any sexier, I'd be dead right now."

"You're just saying that." Grady pulled her hips to his and rocked into her. "I thought that was the reaction that all men got for a half-naked woman."

"Not a shifter. And not me." He pulled back from her, just enough that he could get his fill of seeing her body. "This thing you have on, did you pay much for it? Does it have any sort of special meaning for you?"

"No." She laughed. "I thought it was pretty, but it was

on sale and that was the deciding factor. Nothing much other than that."

Nodding once, he ripped it from her. The silk shredded in his hands, and then he dropped it to the floor. Grady fell to his knees in front of her and did the same to her panties, and then buried his mouth over her hot, heavily scented pussy.

He sucked her hard clit into his mouth and suckled it as he was going to her nipples. Running his hand up her thigh, he slid his fingers into her as he nibbled on her nether lips, fucking her with his tongue. All the while she flooded his mouth with cream, her body rocking into his mouth as he took what she offered. And when she came, her body bowing back, he freed his cock, pulling it from his boxers and fisting himself as she came a second, then a third time.

"Again. Fill me again." Her body responded to his command three more times. She came so hard, so loudly, that he was sure the entire neighborhood could hear. Not that he cared; Grady wanted the world to know that he had his mate. Standing up when she told him she couldn't come again, he lifted her in his arms and laid her on the bed.

Stripping off his pants, he never took his eyes from her. Need was there; it seemed to burn through her to him with every breath they took. And when he was naked, his cock in his hand, he held himself back...he didn't want to hurt her with his need.

"If I come all over you right now, I think I'll be able to make love to you without climaxing the moment I enter you." She sat up and reached for him. "You touch me, love, and I'm going to come. I can hardly hold back as it is."

"Don't hold back, please. I need you." Harper licked her lips as she watched him fist his cock. "When you come, I want to taste it, rub it over my body. I need to feel you marking me."

Grady nodded and grabbed blindly for the post at the end of the bed. It was that or he was going to fall on his ass. As he watched her, sitting there with her mouth open, her eyes closed, he thought of taking her, bending her over the bed and filling her with his cock. Almost as soon as the thought of him filling her with his seed hit his mind, he felt his climax shudder over his body.

His cum touched her mouth, cheeks, and breasts. When she licked her lips again, taking him into her, he cried out and felt his cock jerk hard in his fist. Coming a second time, his body stiff with the release, he knew for as long as he lived, the image of her licking his cum off her lips would be foremost in his mind.

Jerking her up from the bed, his body still hard with need, he told her to bend over, to hold onto the mattress. Slamming into her, holding her hips in his hands, Grady fucked her hard, his body needing to dominate her, to mark her as his own. And when he was close to coming again, he leaned over her and slid his fingers into her soaking pussy and pinched her clit hard. Harper screamed out her release and held his hand to her.

When he was able to move again, he pulled her body up to his. Holding her like this, her back to his chest, Grady explored her breasts, her navel, and even her throat. She was soft and firm at the same time, her breasts full of milk; he wanted to taste her. Turning her around, he took her breast into his mouth and sucked the warm liquid as it slid down his throat.

"Yes, Christ, yes." He lifted her up while he suckled at her breast. "Grady, I'm going to come if you keep that up. Please. Take me."

Grady pressed her against the wall by the bed. Never letting her go, he slid her down so that his cock was at her entrance. He wanted to see her face as he filled her, watch her eyes as he fucked her. Lifting his head from her breast, he kissed her then, and slowly lowered her over him. Grady watched her face.

Rapture. He was sure that was what he was seeing there. Her eyes had darkened; her breaths were hitched. As he slowly entered her, his cock being strangled just a little more with each inch he buried himself in her, he wanted everything. Fucking her slowly, entering a little only to back up a some to take her again, Grady fell in love with his wife again and again as she held him.

"Come for me, my love. I need to see you while you give me all that you are." Her body bowed away from the wall, her face tightened as her body did the same around him. And when she released, he came with her, and they became one person in that moment.

Taking her to the bed when he thought he could walk without falling over, he lay beside her. She slept then, her body relaxed. Grady watched her breaths as they left her body. The way her pulse beat at her throat. Holding her hand in his, he put his finger over the rhythm at her wrist and was glad to feel it was unsteady as his own.

When she turned to him, he kissed her before she could speak. And when he pulled back, she moved toward him, rolling him to his back and laying her head on his chest. Grady held her to him, touching her back, her head, wherever he could touch.

"I'm so happy right now." He said that he was as well. "I never thought that I'd be even close to this point in my life. Ever. I love you for all that you've given me."

He lifted her chin so that he could see her face. "You have no idea how glad I am that you slipped the piece of jewelry on your arm. Thrilled about the fact that Caelin sent me to find you. And that you came to me, with your mind and heart open enough that I could love you as you are. That you've given me a part of you that you created, a son that I will love as much as I do you. For all time."

"Oh Grady, whatever would I have done without you?" He held her, his wife, the other half of his beating heart. The woman that he loved more than he did himself.

Closing his eyes, he let sleep take him. It was a peaceful slipping from being awake to resting. Grady was a happy man.

~~~

Kenton was in his office when Caelin reached out to him. He'd been expecting it for days now, Caelin telling him that another piece had been found. Or that it was coming to an end, someone that had been coming was dead. He so wanted to hear that another mate was coming to his brothers. Smiling, hoping for the best, he asked what piece was coming and who he thought was going to receive it. Kenton stood up when he felt the dragon's fear.

My lord, I wish for you to calm down. Your mind is a jumble at the moment, and I cannot get past it. Kenton sat, his head still going as quickly as his heart. *The woman is coming, as you have surmised, but she is in trouble. More so than any of the other women. I believe the men, the dragon slayers, they are picking up their game.*

Stepping up their game. And is she where we can get to her? Do you know where she is? He said that he did not, only that she was near the piece but hadn't touched it yet. Something occurred to Kenton when he realized what the dragon was saying. *You're getting stronger too, aren't you? I mean, before you*

175

had to have them touch the jewelry to know. You can tell now when they're close.

Yes. I never thought of that, but I think you to be correct. I know that she is within.... Kenton waited while the dragon tried to work out the distance. *She is within several feet of it, but she is moving away now. I think...I cannot tell where she is or the piece, only that it's close to her. Lord Grady or Lady Harper will know; I have faith that they can help better now in which piece is where.*

They can tell, but I've not asked them. I'm afraid, if you want to know the truth. If we go there it might alert whoever is looking for it that they've found the right piece. I guess there are fakes out there that are being chased down as well. Caelin said that was right. *When she touches the piece, what will you know about her? More than with the others, I'm assuming.*

I do not know, but as you have pointed out, I'm stronger for the other sparks of me. Kenton also knew that the parts of the dragon were called sparks. He had no idea why, but the queen had told Grady and Harper and they had no reason not to believe her. *Lord Kenton, I wish for you to be ready. I know that you are a good surgeon, but I think you should need help. Not just at home, but in your offices as well. You are being watched even as we speak.*

We're half way to having all the pieces now, I'm betting that they're worried that once we have them all, we'll be unstoppable. Caelin told him that they would be unstoppable. *I'll work on getting more help, not just with the clinic and hospital, but with the household as well. Everyone will need to step up their game.*

Kenton sat in his office chair and tried to think if he had people watching every avenue of his family. His mom had taken to going to the store recently with one of his brothers or himself. The women, all of them, were pretty strong now because of the addition that Harper brought, but he still asked them to not go out alone. Even Gavin, who was taking some college classes at the local university, was well watched. He thought that while he had everyone covered, he was still missing a lot. He looked up when Grady came in the door.

"I forgot to get a bank." He sounded so panicky that Kenton laughed. "I'm serious. How the hell am I supposed to open today without a bank? Christ, the store is perfect, I have enough employees to have a good day, and no money."

"You do know that you can just go to the regular bank and pick some up?" Grady reminded him it was Sunday. "Oh shit."

"Yeah, oh shit." Kenton pulled out his wallet and reached for his family, telling them what was going on. They were all headed to the new computer store anyway, and he had them bring all the cash they had. "I have about seventy bucks myself. Harper said she has about a hundred. No one carries cash anymore."

They made their way to Dragon Computers. There was a line along the sidewalk that made Grady pause in mid step. Grabbing his brother's arm, he led him to the back of the store. There was a thick bank bag on the counter when they went to the showroom. He started laughing when he read the note.

"You have the most intelligent wife of all time, Grady. Here, she left you a bank bag and note." He read it aloud. "'I knew that you were really busy, so I stopped by the bank to make you a first day register. If you've already done it, then that's fine. I'll take it back when I get there. Good luck today. And I love you.'"

"Christ, I love her." Grady put the money that he'd gotten from the family, all seventy dollars' worth of it, as well as the thousand-dollars that Harper had set up, into the register. They were in business, as far as Kenton could see.

Kenton helped him get things set up as employees began

to come in to help out. He knew that his brother had been training them on items in the store, and he was glad to see them going around and re-familiarizing themselves with things. Kenton knew that this was going to be a success for Grady, and was glad for it.

Kenton asked Grady where Harper was today. "She wanted to go to the studio and work. I guess she has some ideas, and it was making her a little nutty not being able to work. Did you know that she has this big show coming up soon? Jorden and her are also setting up the gallery. Some of her things were shipped from her home last week."

"I saw some of her work when Jorden was opening the crates. Christ, I'd love to have a couple of them." He would too, if he could convince her to give him a nice family discount. "Do you suppose if I asked her, she'd do something for the pack house? Also, for Kurt and his new mate as a housewarming gift."

"I'm sure she'd do it. She's going to make me something for the front window too. I told her that it didn't have to be big, but she had this faraway look on her face, and I knew she'd already designed it as well as the colors." Grady laughed. "Remember how Jorden would get when he had a painting that was forming in his head?"

"Yes. He was cranky until he got to start on it. Well, that isn't the word that described him, but he was very vocal about needing to begin it." Grady asked if he was ready. "Yes, open up and let's get this started."

The rest of the family had come to help as well. Kenton hadn't been sure that they'd be needed, but he wanted to support his little brother in this. But almost as soon as the doors were opened, he knew that they were going to require more help. There were at least four hundred people coming in and ready to shop. Grady had hit the nail on the head for this business.

Around noonish, things started to slow enough that Mom was able to go and get sandwiches. Kenton sat at one of the little tables that had been set up for Wi-Fi usage and closed his eyes. Almost as soon as he did he was being poked by someone, and looked up at Douglas, their attorney.

"Don't freak out." He shook his head. "Good. I've just been notified the company that Grady purchased all his inventory from is coming here to take it back." Kenton stood up and he felt his dragon move along his skin. "You're not supposed to be freaking out, remember?"

"I do. They sure have planned this out perfectly, haven't they? Have you told Grady?" Douglas said he was hoping he'd come with him when he did. "Chicken."

"Yes, I am. His dragon is bigger than yours, and he scares me with this new freaky thing he can do." Douglas asked him what he meant, and wondered how he'd figured out about the way he could tell the future. "That strength thing. Christ, I saw him in town the other day and he lifted up that truck of his and moved it away from the sidewalk like it was nothing. That scared the shit out of me."

"You should see him when he's angry. He's like that big green guy we watched on television when we were younger." Douglas backed away. "I'm joking. He won't hurt you. We all have it to a degree, but you're right, Grady's dragon is much bigger and stronger. He also has control over him a little more than the rest of us. I'm not sure how that works yet."

"Yeah, well I hope he has great control. I don't want to have to explain why attorneys for this company, as well as their CEOs, ended up as char in a computer store." Kenton laughed but Douglas didn't. And that made Kenton laugh all the harder. "You laugh now, buddy, but these people mean to take him for everything he has."

They found Grady in the office. He wasn't on the phone but was having a conversation. When Kenton asked him what was going on, he showed him the wireless mike and ear set. He was apparently well aware that the company, Electrical Outlet, was coming. Grady was talking to someone about transcripts. A few minutes later the machine, which Kenton had assumed was a copier but was actually a fax machine, started working. Grady disconnected the call and looked at them.

"The trucker that day, do you remember what he said about a third party recording every conversation that came into their offices?" Kenton nodded. "Well, if you need a copy, say for something that might have been said when you called in, they'll send you a faxed copy of the conversation at no charge. Nice of them, don't you think?"

"They told you that they didn't make mistakes." Grady nodded and smiled. "When did you get so smart?"

"I've always been smart, you just never looked before." Grady stood up when Opal came to say there was someone to see him. "You can come along if you'd like to see how much more awesome I am than you think now."

Kenton said he'd not miss this for the world. Douglas asked if he was able to watch and Grady handed him the printout. Kenton could see that not only was it a transcript of what Grady had said, but also what the trucker, Miles James, had said when he'd called about the mistake. There was also a copy of the billing that both Miles and Grady had signed.

"Mr. McCade, I'm afraid we're going to have to ask you to shut your doors. Your inventory is considered stolen." The man's voice carried around the packed store, just as he'd hoped it would. But instead of people looking at Grady like he was a thief, they looked murderously at the man who spoke. "You received this inventory into your shop nefariously. I'm afraid we're going to have to either get the full amount for it, or you'll to have to close up so that we can take an inventory and you'll pay us for whatever is sold when we take it back."

"No. I don't think so. I called, you said you didn't make mistakes." The man said that everyone did. "Yes. And when I pointed that out to your company they said they were professionals and that they took great pride in their on-time delivery, as well as their merchandise being top notch. I tried to explain to them that I had no problem with either the timeliness of the delivery nor the merchandise, but the pricing of each piece, not to mention the amount I was sent. I was told to basically shut up, and that mistakes were never made by your company."

"I cannot believe that anyone would—" He was cut off when Douglas handed him the transcripts. Instead of reading them, however, he handed them off to the person next to him. "Anyone can have things printed up, Mr. McCade. If you're going to give me trouble, I'm afraid that I'll have to call in the police. I had hoped that we could do this quietly and without—"

"You mean quietly like you've just done? Coming into my shop on opening day and announcing to everyone that I have stolen merchandise? You mean that sort of quiet?" The man flushed brightly. "You should have all your ducks in a row before coming into a place that I own."

The man next to him holding the transcripts asked to speak to the attorney. When he tried to brush him off, he jerked him around and handed him a single sheet. Apparently whatever was there made both men pale.

As the two men conferred, Kenton reached out to his brother and asked him what had happened. Grady just laughed, the sound of it so happy that Kenton found himself joining in.

Mom. She called the company on Friday and talked to their company president. She told him how lovely it was that someone in his company had thought themselves to be flawless, and that their perfection was going to make her son's new company a great success. I guess he was none too pleased to find out about the mistake they didn't make. Kenton said he'd not be. *Well, apparently I was told to call him directly when one of his attorneys showed up. Mom gave me the number a few days ago. And when I knew these yo-yos were coming, I gave him a call. He told me that should I need any more supplies, since I was so honest in the first place, to call him again. I guess I have a buddy in the industry now. Anyway, he wrote a note at the bottom of the printout of my conversation with them. As well as the trucker's.*

And do you know what it said? Grady just winked at him when the attorneys came back from their little pow-wow.

"Mr. McCade, it seems that you are owed an apology for our coming here. And how you were treated when you called in to first report that we made a mistake." Grady said he was glad that they'd finally figured that out. "Yes. Mr. Winchell has told us to let you know if you ever need anything, and he said anything at all, we'll be delivering it right to your door even if we have to bring it to you in our own cars."

"That won't be necessary, but I do appreciate it." Grady looked around the room, then back at the people. "If you'd like to have some refreshments, please help yourself. My grand opening is a great success thanks to your company."

After the men walked away, Douglas patted Grady on his back and told him well played. Kenton was really proud of his little brother and told him so. The rest of the afternoon was busy, but Kenton could see that Grady was much more relaxed about it.

CHAPTER 13

Gabe moved along the hospital ward. She was beyond exhausted today, and couldn't remember the last time she'd had not just a good night's sleep, but a decent meal too. This shit needed to stop soon or she was going to be dead before she was forty. As she entered her office, she saw the brightly wrapped box on her desk as well as the little man sitting in the chair across from her seat. Going in and taking off her lab coat, she cleared her throat and started talking.

"It's not my birthday, so that can't be it. Nor do I have a husband, so there is no anniversary that I forgot either." He stood up and tipped his hat at her. "I don't know you, so you either explain to me why you're in my office — that I know I locked before I left.... I think it was two days ago — or I'm going to have your dapper little self thrown out on your ass."

"Doctor Gabriela Nola?" She didn't confirm nor deny his query. "I'm Lucas Peterson. You don't know me, but I work for...or I worked for a man by the name of Theodore Waterson. You won't know him any more than you do me, but I'll explain."

She sat at her desk and wanted to kick her shoes off, but if she had to get rid of this man she didn't want to look unprofessional to the staff when she did it. Gabe looked at the box again and saw her name on the pretty ribbon that hung from the top.

"You left this here?" He nodded and sat down, laying his hat on the seat next to him. She thought of dragons and faeries. She had no idea why that popped into her head, but it did. "What are you doing in my office, Mr. Peterson? And who is Mr. Waterson?"

"Yes, yes. I should move on. Mr. Waterson was a collector, you could say. Not a hoarder as they portray on the television, but a man who had an eye for the older, finer things in life. He had a great many things in his estate. Most of them have been gathered over his very long and productive life." She told him to get on with it. "Yes, I'm sorry. I know that you must be tired. Mr. Waterson died a few months back. His estate, like those of so many people of his era, was large and entailed. It has taken me a while to sort through the many things that he wished to be given away. Even more items that need sold off and donated. This box, the one there, is only a part of what you are to receive."

"You said that I don't know him." Mr. Peterson said that was right. "Yet he left me something, a present it looks like, and you say there is more. I don't want it. I don't know him, and it's weird that he is leaving me something. I'm sorry to have wasted your time."

"The dragon wishes you to open the box." Her entire body froze at the word. Dragon. She put her hands under her legs to keep them from shaking, her feet planted firmly on the carpet so she'd not run. "He knows who you are and what you mean to his wellbeing."

"I don't know what you're talking about." She was pretty sure that not only didn't he believe her, but he knew just what the dragon had told her a few nights ago. "I think it's time that

186

you left."

"Mr. Waterson spoke to the dragon as well. He told him that you'd not believe in such things, but he said that you would have to…the world and its people are depending on you to believe." Gabe started to stand but his next words stopped her cold. "He said to tell you that he knows where the dragon is."

"No."

Mr. Peterson nodded and began speaking to her. He might have been using English or even some of the other dozen or so languages that she knew, but she was terrified, her body hard pressed now to even remain upright. Sitting down, she looked at the box and told him what she'd heard that night.

"I was coming from the emergency department. I had had to call the death of a young boy, no more than ten. His father had killed him. Just put a gun to his head and shot him there because he'd been into his things. What sort of things would a boy need to get into to have his own father murder him?" Mr. Peterson said he was sorry, or something along those lines. "He was dead; we all could see that. A part of his brain was laying on the gurney beside him. His body was cold; his eyes, however, were wide open. I was just ready to call it when he suddenly grabbed my arm and looked at me."

"Go on, Gabriela, tell me what he said to you." She shook her head, still not believing that he'd spoken. The part of his brain that used motor skills such as speaking and even breathing was gone. "Gabriela?"

"He said that the dragon was coming. That I should do everything within my power to help. Then he put out his hand and there in the palm was this dragon, a large blue and golden one with his wings wide open. The boy said once again that I was to help in any way I could; that the dragon, he needed me."

"And everyone else, they didn't see this?" She said that she'd asked and they thought her over worked. She told Mr. Peterson that she thought that as well. "But something else happened, didn't it? You know that he was telling the truth."

"A few days later, after the boy had been taken away, someone left a note that I was to go find the dragons." Gabe looked at the drawer where she'd put the small dragon, and the note that was written by the most beautiful hand. With her own trembling hard enough that she could barely open the drawer, she pulled out the small glass dragon and held it up. Colors, different shades of blue, danced around her office. What freaked her out even now was that there was no sunlight behind her. The overhead light in her office, like before, was off. There wasn't any way that the light sparks could be doing what they were now.

"He was real, my lady. As are the dragons." Shaking her head, she put it back in the drawer and asked about the gift. "It is from Mr. Waterson. He knew who you were the moment that his grandson, the boy that you tried to save, spoke to him."

"When?" He said just after his death. "No, that's not possible. He was dead. I don't know what sort of game you're playing here, but the dead don't talk to the living."

He stood up and so did she. "The gift is for you. You may take it if you wish or not. I have brought it to you, but I should point out that it comes with great risk, you taking the gift. There are people even now looking for the person who has such a priceless bequest as the one you have been given."

Then he was gone. Not just left the room where she was, but just gone. Getting up, she ignored the gift with the blue and gold wrapper on it, and the equally bright ribbon that had her name, Gabriela, spelled down it. Instead she moved around her office trying to ascertain whether or not she should have a CAT scan done to her head and her hearing checked. There was nothing in her office to indicate someone had been speaking to her about a dragon.

Sitting back at her desk, she moved the box aside with a pen. She wasn't going to touch it, she told herself. Not ever if she could help it. Pulling the first of many files to her, she began to work on them.

Her goal was to get them completed, then she'd go home. Tomorrow was her first day off in a month, and she was going to use it catching up on everything she'd let slide. Sleep, laundry, sleep. Napping too if she could work it in, as well as sleep. Smiling, Gabe set to work.

Nearly three hours later she looked up from the last of the files. It had been an accident…three people dead and fourteen more injured. She was writing up her work that had been done on the man who had died before even coming to her when someone knocked on her door. She might have ignored it, but she'd left it open so they knew she was here.

"We have a problem." Gabe told her that she was out of the problem department today. "Yeah, well, a cop was just brought in via life flight. He's been hurt pretty badly, and Wilson is a no-show again."

"Christ, I've been on duty for over fifty straight hours. I can't do this anymore." June, the nurse from ER, only nodded. "I'm giving my notice in the morning. I cannot keep this up."

Gabe grabbed her lab coat and followed her out of the room. She really was going to do it this time. As she entered the small room to help, she was working out the resignation in her mind. Yes, she was done with this shit as of today.

~~~

Grady was coming even as he woke. His body had been poised for it for some time, it seemed. As he released, coming fully awake as he did so, he realized that Harper was riding him. He sat up and took her breast in his mouth and suckled.

"I was wondering if you were ever going to join me." He grabbed her hips to slow her down. "No, I'm so close now that if you keep touching me, I'm going to come."

"You're so greedy. I want to enjoy you again." He rolled her to her back and fucked her hard for several strokes. "Harper, if you want to wake me like this every morning, you just might kill me."

"But what a way to die." He ran his tongue along her throat to the pulse there. Nipping at her none too gently, he moved back to her breast and enjoyed the warm milk that seemed to be in great abundance there. "Grady, leave some for Shawn. Talk about greedy."

He was too. Not just for what she offered him, but for what he saw in her eyes. Love. She loved him as much as he did her. He brought her twice, once by biting her throat then the other just loving her as hard as he could. But he was far from finished with her as he made love to her with his hands, touching her everywhere he could reach.

"Please, you're killing me." He laughed as he made his way down her body to her pussy. His pleasing her was only just beginning, and he planned on savoring every part of her. Grady was going to take his time too.

Her pussy was soaking wet, her lips swollen from his cock. As he nibbled on her flesh, he showed her images of what he was going to do with her. Every time she came, several times in fact, he would start all over, bring her to peak as often as he could until she was limp under his body.

"I love the way you scream out my name. How you get

that little hitch in your voice while you're doing it." Harper smacked him on the shoulder. "You do. You should see the way your eyes sort of go all glassy. How your nipples get so hard, I can't wait to bite them." Grady licked her ribs, each of them, then moved to the other side. "You taste like what I think heaven would. Soft and creamy. Just a bit of spice that makes me feel like you're perfect for me."

"Grady, please? I need to have you inside of me again." He made his way down her legs, touching her knees and the backs of her calves. Grady rubbed her ankles, her toes, and then kissed each of them. "You're going to pay for this."

"I hope so. Besides, you're the one that woke me up by sitting on my cock. I think it's only fair that I make you suffer as well." He laughed when she slapped out at him. "I think you're the best thing that has ever happened to me, love."

"Remember that when I have to visit you in jail. I think there's a crime for making your wife suffer like this." He said that he was pretty sure he was safe. "You think? Just wait, payback is a bitch."

Moving up her body again, he kissed her navel, suckling at the small indentation there. Her hips were smoothed over, her ribs counted again. And when he took her mouth, sliding his cock deep into her, she wrapped her legs over his and he rode her slowly this time.

"I love you with all that I am." She kissed him then, pulling his head to hers and showing with words how much she loved him too. When he moved into her again, sliding in and out of her sheath, Grady pulled her hands up over her head and wrapped them around the bedpost. "You're distracting me."

"I'm dying is what I am." He kissed her again and felt her fingers wrap around his neck to his shoulders. "Hurry, Grady. Hurry and finish me."

He did then, feeling, no doubt, what she did. They were about to have company. Fucking her hard, taking her twice more before he emptied himself into her, he felt his dragon move over his skin and he leaned down and bit her on the marks at her upper arm.

They both came again, crying out their releases to anyone within earshot. When he kissed her, pounding her through another powerful climax, Grady felt the moment that something touched his arm in the same place that she'd been marked. Without even looking, he knew that he now carried the sigil that she did.

Dropping down on top of her, he rolled to his back, taking her with him. As they laid there, out of breath and their hearts racing, he had to smile. Christ, she really was going to murder him if they kept it up like this. Even when he was younger, he hadn't come several times like he did now. Holding her to him, Grady asked her if she was all right.

"Yes. I'm wonderful as a matter of fact. I have some things I'm going to be working on today that have me really excited." She got up and went to the bathroom, still talking to him about her day. "Jorden and I have been talking to some promoters, and we're going to have a grand opening sometime in January. I think I'll be ready by then."

Taking a shower with her took longer than he knew it should have. But he couldn't get enough of touching her, and he loved the way her hands seemed to be everywhere on his body. When they were dressed and went downstairs to have breakfast, neither of them were surprised to find Vance there. He was home again. But for how long, Grady wondered.

"I have some information for you that I'd like to tell you now." Vance sat down when introduced to Harper, and then was given a large platter of food. "I've been able to locate two of the pieces that you told me about. One of them belongs to a doctor named Gabe Nola. You know him?"

"No, but it's a she, not a man. She'll be coming here soon. And the other piece? Have you been able to locate its owner yet?" Vance shook his head. "You'll find it. I'm sure of it."

"Do you suppose this doc, she's my mate?" Grady said that he didn't know, that part was blocked from him. "I don't need a mate, Grady. I have enough trouble as it is."

"I'm sorry about that, Vance. I wish I could tell you something." He could, so could Harper, but they decided to keep it to themselves. It was better that way. "When do you leave again? I'm assuming that you're only here for a little while before you take off once more?"

"I have a month." Grady nodded and asked him if he'd seen a doctor of his own yet. "I have. Medic said I was doing just fine."

He was pretty sure that he hadn't, but Grady said nothing. Vance, now that he knew what he did for a living, was not a man to fuck with. Not even if you were his brother like he was. He'd seen things, done things, that would have given most men he knew nightmares. Hell, more than likely they'd be put away for a very long time in some nuthouse in a room with padded walls.

Harper left them a little while later, inviting Vance to stay with them while he was home. Vance, like the rest of them, had a home, thanks to Emma, but Grady had no idea which one Vance had ended up with. The man was a loner as well as a hard man to get to know. Even being his brother, Grady knew that few of them were aware of what he did for a living, and why when he came home, he was so beaten.

"I experienced my dragon last week. This new thing, being stronger, did you know that it has other perks as well?"

Grady asked him what sort of perks. Instead of answering him, Vance pulled a long switchblade from his boot and cut it across his palm. The blood seeped, but only for a second before it disappeared with the cut. "I can cut myself just about anywhere and it heals that fast. And here is something really freaky, I was shot and the bullet popped right out of my wound."

"Wound where?" Vance didn't say anything, so Grady looked. "Christ, Vance. You need to stay safer for us. I don't know what I'd do without you."

"Live. Go on. I would. It's not like I'm here much. Would anyone even care?" It hurt him, all the way to his core, to hear his bother say something like that. "Anyway, I have a few things I need for you to do for me. My house is being set up for security, and I'd like for you to do the computer work. I have some connections that I want you to link it to, and nowhere else."

"I can do that. Also, I picked up your mail yesterday. You should really do something about having it done on a regular basis. Milly called when it was overflowing. I can pick it up for you when I get mine if you want. I don't think she'll care if I ask for it." He said he'd give him a key before he left. "When does the work begin?"

"Last week. I have several different crews working on it; no one knows what the other is doing in this." He didn't ask him why, but assumed that Vance wouldn't tell him anyway. "I also have some things being delivered. Guns and such. Will you store them until I return again?"

"You're going to be here for a month, though, right?" He said he was. "Can you tell me why this time? Are you hurt?"

"No. Not hurt." Grady nodded when his brother said no more. "I'm doing this because I'm good at what I do, Grady.

Not for any kind of glory or some shit like that."

"Since I have no idea what you do, I'll assume you're right. But we miss you." Vance said nothing. "The jewelry, it's going to be complete soon. You know that will involve you, don't you?"

"If it does then we're all fucked. I'm not going to be a part of the McCades finding a new bride group. I can't do that." Grady asked him why. Again without answering, he stood up and pulled his shirt off his head. He saw things on his brother's body that terrified him in their violence. "I'm not the kind of man that a woman, no matter what she says, can stand to look at."

"Vance, I'm so sorry." He was too. Not just for the pain that his brother had endured when he'd been cut, stabbed, and what appeared to be shot to fuck on his body, but also the numerous scars that he was sure he couldn't see. Vance had led a very hard and difficult life.

After he left, telling him that he'd be at his house, Grady made his way to work. He was going to show off his dragon tonight to Harper. Take her on a small ride as well. He was excited for that, but also nervous. He'd never flown before, not even in a plane. And he was afraid of hurting her by dropping her or something.

His store was open by the time he got there. Opal had agreed to stay on as his assistant manager, so that part was nice. Kurt was still pissed off at him about Opal, but he knew that he'd come around sooner or later. Opal and her little girls were living in the house that Kurt had purchased, so he knew that he'd made some headway in convincing her to let him care for her. Life, he knew, was about to get very interesting for Kurt and Opal.

He was just sitting down at his desk when he closed his

eyes to center himself. The image that popped into his head nearly had him jumping up and running. Instead, he sat very still and watched as each detail burned itself into his mind.

A fire. A shooting. There was blood everywhere, and the sounds of screaming. He hadn't found the source of it as yet, but he watched as things played out in his head. As he reached blindly for a pen, he started writing down some of the people he could see. Not their names—he didn't know them—but what they looked like, marks on their bodies that he could recognize later if need be.

Then he saw her, the woman. She was dressed in a long gown, her hair long since fallen from whatever style she'd had it in. There were fire trucks pulling into where she was, police were shouting at someone behind her. As she moved from body to body, her dress becoming more stained, he saw her face, the grim determination that she had.

She's a doctor. He told Harper that she was correct, he thought. *Where is that? I've never seen that house before.*

He said that he hadn't either, but he thought he should know it. Abandoned, his mind screamed at him. The house was abandoned, somewhere. But he knew it too was different, it's roof new, the paint fresh. Even the grass had been trimmed, the hedges as well.

As he watched the woman, mindful of the things he might need to know later, Grady felt his heart hurt, and his hands stop moving, when a man came up behind the woman and shot her in the back of the head. The images disappeared as soon as he realized she was dead.

"Christ, what the fuck was that?" He didn't know, was actually afraid to as he sat there, but he looked down at his notes and realized he did. This was Gabriela Nola, and she needed them.

Before You Go...

HELP AN AUTHOR

write a review

THANK YOU!

Share your voice and help guide other readers to these wonderful books. Even if it's only a line or two your reviews help readers discover the author's books so they can continue creating stories that you'll love. Login to your favorite retailer and leave a review. Thank you.

Kathi Barton, author of the bestselling series Force of Nature, lives in Nashport, Ohio with her husband Paul. In addition to writing full time Kathi likes to spend time with her eight grandkids, three children and three children-in-laws. She writes to relax and have fun.

Her muse, a cross between Jimmy Stewart and Hugh Jackman brings them to life for her readers in a way that has them coming back time and again for more. Her favorite genre is paranormal romance with a great deal of spice. You can visit Kathi on line and drop her an email if you'd like. She loves hearing from her fans. aaronskiss@gmail.com.

Follow Kathi on her blog: http://kathisbartonauthor.blogspot.com/